SLEEPY TIME SPACE TALES

. . . .

Bedtime Stories from Beyond the Blue Skies

By: Dr. Ronald L. Washington, J.D.

Mother Hall,
Thank you for your
Spirit and support.
You are a great
lady.
Ronald L. Washington

ISBN:1467959502

ISBN-13:9781467959506

DEDICATION

This book of stories is first dedicated to my children; Oni, Rahn, Alexis and Ryan. Without you in my life I would not have had the inspiration to write these tales and continue to work on them. I love you all dearly.

I also dedicate this book to Barack Obama, Steve Harvey and Michael Baisden. All of you, in the examples you have set, and many myriad ways have encouraged me to continue to work hard to make the dream of this book come true.

CONTENTS

ACKNOWLEDGMENTS

I want to acknowledge and give honor to God for all that he has given me the talent to do and for the gift of my brothers; Saul, David, James and Elvin and my beautiful and brave sister, Brenda. By your fine examples, you have all taught me invaluable life lessons, and I know will forever be a part of my life's successes.

I especially want to acknowledge and thank God for my sainted mother Missionary Lorraine Stephens Washington Hunt for being the constant spark in my life-long fire for wisdom and wonder. Mom, I hope to continue to make you proud and know you continue to guide my path from Heaven.

PERCIRON PAYS THE PRICE

One cosmic summer, Perciron from the planet Pridon sat with his grandfather. His grandfather suggested that they go shopping together. Perciron loved to go shopping. The two of them went outside and climbed into Grandfather's space car and were soon on their way. After a short ride, the two of them could see the gleaming metal buildings of the city. Grandfather told Perciron that he wanted to go to the Computer Center and look at the new robots. On arriving there, they went inside and were greeted with a mechanical "Good day," from the robot salesman behind the counter. Grandfather went over and began to talk to the robot salesman while

Perciron wandered around looking at all the wonderful things in the store.

Everything looked so exciting and new! Over in the far corner was a little red skycle light. Perciron thought how good it would look on his skycle. Perciron wanted that light. He knew he couldn’t buy it, because he had no money. He didn’t want to ask Grandfather, because Grandfather had given him money yesterday, and he had spent it all. Grandfather also told him he had to learn how to save money.

He wanted the light so bad. It would be just perfect on his skycle. The light was just small enough to put into his pants’ pocket. He knew he would be stealing, and he knew stealing was wrong, but he just couldn't seem to help himself. So, he grabbed the light and stuffed it in his pocket. For a minute, he thought about changing his mind. He almost did the right thing and put the stolen light back, but he didn't.

Then he heard Grandfather calling him.

“I’m here,” yelled Perciron running over to where Grandfather and the robot were standing.

“Time to go,” said Grandfather. “I’m not going to buy anything today. I may come back tomorrow, and I will let you come with me. You have been such a good boy today. I may even give you some money.”

Perciron knew he had not been good, but he did not say anything and they walked through the sliding doors and out of the store.

As they glided along the moving sidewalk, Grandfather looked down at Perciron.

“Perciron, look at me,” he said.

Perciron did.

“What is that purple spot on your pants?”

“What purple spot?” asked Perciron.

“On your pants’ pocket, where that lump is.” What do you have in your pocket?” asked Grandfather.

For the first time, Perciron noticed that there was a round dark purple spot on the pocket he had put the red light in!

Then Perciron tried to lie.

“Oh, it must be grape juice, and I have a ball in my pocket,” he said.

Grandfather knew Perciron did not have any grape juice. He also knew that Perciron did not bring a ball to the Computer Center.

“You took something from the Computer Center, didn't you? Let’s see what you have in your pocket.”

Sadly, Perciron reached into his pocket and brought out the little red skycle light.

“Where did you get that?”

“I took it from the Computer Center.”

"Did a robot salesman give it to you?"

"No."

"I know you didn't have any money to buy it, so you must have taken it without asking. Did you?"

"Yes," the little boy said, almost crying.

"Well then, Perciron that was a very bad thing to do. You know better than to steal. Haven't I taught you that stealing is wrong? I am very angry and ashamed of you. Let's go home and decide what we're going to do about this."

Perciron began to cry, and he cried all the way back home in the space car.

When they got inside, Grandfather told Perciron to sit down. He told the little boy again and again and again how wrong it was to take things from other people.

He asked him how he'd feel if someone took something from him. Perciron said he wouldn't like that at all. Grandfather then told Perciron he would have to return to the

Computer Center and pay for the skycle light.

"I promise not to steal or do anything wrong again, Grandfather, but I don't have any money to pay for the light," Perciron replied. He felt very bad inside. It felt like he had a stomach ache. He didn't like Grandfather being angry and ashamed of him. He wanted Grandfather to be proud of him. He knew he would never steal again.

"Well, if you get your piggy bank I'm sure you will find the money," Grandfather said.

"But, I was saving that money to buy a new skycle! I almost had enough in my piggy bank. If I pay for the light, I'll have even less money for my new skycle!" Perciron replied.

"That's right. That is what you must learn. Everything has a price. If you want something, you have to pay for it. If you don't have any money, you should work to get it. No matter what you want in life, you have to pay the price for it."

Grandfather then took Perciron and the piggy bank to his space car, and soon they were zooming back to the city. When they arrived at the Computer Center, Grandfather waited outside and told Perciron to go inside, confess what he had done, and pay for the light.

As he walked inside, Perciron held the money tightly. He didn't want to let it go, but he knew he had to do the right thing.

The robot salesman greeted him as he reached the counter.

"I was a bad boy, and I stole this skycle light from your store. I am sorry for what I did, and I will never do it again. I came back to pay for it."

The robot salesman looked at Perciron and smiled. Then he began to laugh. "Why did you want the light?" he asked.

"I wanted it for my skycle. I thought it would look very good on the new one I'm going to buy when I save enough money," Perciron said sadly.

"You were a bad boy," said the robot, "but a bad boy can be a good boy, if he wants to be. You want to be a good boy. That is good. Since you tried to do the right thing by paying for the light, I am going to let you keep it for free. And, you know what? I am going to give you another one for your new skycle."

Perciron couldn't believe it! He smiled widely and said "thanks," over and over again as he ran out the door to Grandfather's space car. He got there so fast he felt like he was running on air.

"Look what he gave me, Grandfather, two lights! Aren't they nice?" Perciron yelled.

Grandfather looked. Perciron had two shiny red skycle lights, and his full piggy bank.

"He gave them to you because you tried to do the right thing and pay for the light?"

"Yes!"

"Aren't you glad you went back and told the truth?"

"Am I ever!" exclaimed Perciron.

"You see, it is always best to do the right thing."

As he and Grandfather flew back home, Perciron looked forward to a bright future and always being mindful of his lesson; honesty is the best policy.

MARZONA AND THE MAGIC COIN

On a far off planet lives a girl named Marzona. She lives with her mother and father in an old abandoned spaceship. Once they were very poor, and they barely had enough money to live.

Marzona's father was a painter, and he painted many beautiful pictures, but no one was buying his pictures anymore. Her mother wrote beautiful songs and sang, but no one wanted to hear beautiful songs anymore. So, they became poorer and poorer and poorer.

Before long were forced to go into the city and sell everything they had piece by piece. First, they sold the TV, then the DVD player, the computer, their space car, just about everything. In no time, all they had very few things left of any value, and Marzona's parents began to worry a lot about what to do next.

One day Marzona's mother came to her room.

"Your father is sick, Marzona," she said. "He has not eaten in a very long time, because he wanted you and me to have the food. And now we must get him some medicine to make him strong again. The only thing we have left to sell is your skycle. We didn't want to sell it, because we gave it to you for your birthday. But, we have nothing else."

Marzona really loved her skycle, but she loved her father even more. Still, she was sad when she agreed that the only thing they could do to save her father was to sell her skycle.

"You will have to be a big girl and take the skycle into the city and sell it. Sam Serpentanian's Skycle Shop will probably give you a good price for it, but make sure you come right home as soon as you have the money," her mother said.

Marzona agreed and went outside and flew off on her skycle.

When she reached the city, she guided the skycle to Sam Serpentanian's Skycle Shop. It was the same place her parents had brought it from. But, Sam Serpentanian told her that he did not want to buy the skycle back. Marzona begged him to buy it back so that she would have money to buy medicine for her father. Sam Serpentanian only laughed at her in his snake-sounding voice and threw Marzona out.

Marzona sat outside of Sam Serpentanian's Skycle Shop and began to cry. What would she tell her mother? How could she save her father? It all seemed quite hopeless.

Just then a kind-looking old woman dressed in beautiful clothes spoke to Marzona.

"Why are you crying little girl?" she asked.

Marzona told the old woman about her father and how her mother had sent her to the city to sell her skycle, but Sam Serpentanian refused to buy it back.

"I have just what you need," said the old woman. Reaching into her pocket, she pulled out what looked like an ordinary brown penny.

"This coin is magic," she said. "If you place it in your yard and wish very hard, it will give you a clue to make your wish come true. Just give me your skycle and I will give you this Magic Coin, and if your wish does not come true, I'll give the skycle back to you."

Marzona did not know why, but she trusted the old woman, so she handed over the skycle and took the coin and put it in her pocket.

The old woman took the skycle and flew off and since Marzona had no other way, she began to walk home. She did not get very far before a space bus flew by, loaded with people.

The driver stopped and asked Marzona why she was walking. Marzona explained that her skycle was gone, and she had no other way. The kind driver thought it was too dangerous for a little girl to be walking outside the city by herself, so he gave Marzona a free ride home.

Marzona's mother was standing in the door of their spaceship when she saw Marzona climb from the loaded space bus. Since Marzona had not come back on the skycle, her mother guessed that she had sold it, and now they would have money to buy medicine. She was very happy.

"I see you sold the skycle," Marzona's mother said with a smile.

"Well, yes, sort of," Marzona said.

"What do you mean, sort of?" her mother asked. "Where is it? Where is the money?"

Marzona reached into her pocket and pulled out the Magic Coin. Before she could explain what it was, her mother began to yell.

"What is this? A penny? You sold your skycle for a penny? You are a very smart girl. Surely, you could not have done something so dumb! What can we buy with a penny? Nothing!"

Marzona tried to explain about the kind old lady and how the coin was really magic, but her mother didn't want to hear it. She was so angry that she took the coin from Marzona and threw it into the yard and sent the little girl to bed.

That night, while everyone was fast asleep the coin began to glow. It got brighter and brighter until it looked like daylight outside! Then a giant hole began to open in the ground beneath the Magic Coin. It was so deep it seemed to have no bottom. Next, the Magic Coin began turning into a ladder that stretched down into the hole until the end of it was no longer visible.

Then it got dark outside again and all of the light from the Magic Coin was now glowing from the ladder and that light filled the hole. What was once a Magic Coin was now a large glowing hole with a long glowing ladder in it!

That night Marzona had cried herself to sleep as she wished over and over that they would be able to somehow get medicine for her father.

But, she had not slept well so when she woke up it was not quite morning and the sun was not yet up.

Through the open window of her room, Marzona could see the strange light coming from the hole. She got up and ran outside. When she saw the glowing hole and the long glowing ladder, she knew that the coin was magic after all!

She decided not to wake her parents and see what was down in the hole.

She climbed down the ladder. Down, down, down until at

last she reached the bottom. She stepped off onto the ground.

She was surprised at how much light there was. Off in the distance, she saw a mysterious golden palace sitting on top of a golden hill.

She decided to go to the palace and see if someone there could tell her where she could get what she wished for. When she reached the door, she saw that it was only big enough for someone her size, or smaller. She guessed that a child must live here and felt a little better about being way down there in such a strange place. She knocked and waited.

When the door opened, there stood a grown woman who was shorter than Marzona. Her head was very large and seemed too big for her small round body.

"What do you want, girl?" she demanded.

"I am looking for the place where I'm supposed to get my wish," answered Marzona. "Is this it?"

"What are you talking about, girl?" the little round

woman asked. “There are no wishes here.”

“But, I was led here by the Magic Coin and the lady I got the Magic Coin from said it would lead me to the place where I could get my wish.”

“Coin? What Magic Coin? I don’t know what you are talking about. There are no wishes here, and you had better leave before my husband returns. He is a Demon Drago, and Demon Dragos love to eat little girls for breakfast!” said the woman.

“Please, don’t make me leave,” begged Marzona. “I don’t want to go home without my wish. It must be around here somewhere. Maybe you can help me find it. Maybe it’s in another palace!”

“There are no other palaces,” said the woman. “This is the only palace in the land.”

“Then my wish has to be here!” exclaimed Marzona. The old woman said I would find it, if I wished very hard, and I did. The Magic Coin turned into a Magic Ladder and I climbed down the Magic Ladder, and now I'm here. Please, let me in!"

The little woman saw how badly Marzona wanted to come in, and she felt sorry for the little girl.

"Come on in," she said, "but you are taking a big chance. I will let you look around so that you'll know that there are no wishes here."

She led Marzona to a small room with small furniture in it. It looked like a big doll house.

As soon as they sat down, there was the sound of footsteps coming.

"It's my husband, the Demon Drago." said the woman. "He'll eat you alive, if he catches you here. Quick, hide in this closet and be very quiet." Marzona barely had time to get the door closed when in stepped the Demon Drago!

He stood in the middle of the room and looked around.

"Like grass in the springtime and flowers in bloom, the air is filled with a little girl's perfume. Bring her to me, I will have her, I will. I want to make her my morning meal!" He roared in a voice that seemed too big for his short body.

"There is no little girl here," his wife said to him in a scared voice. "Sit down. Let me get you something cool to drink." Through a crack in the closet door, Marzona watched the Demon Drago guzzle his drink. He looked like a little boy with a huge head. His feet looked like they belonged on a giant. After he finished the drink, he put the glass in this mouth and chewed it into little pieces!

Marzona could almost feel him chewing her like that, and she was even more afraid.

When the Demon Drago had swallowed the last bits of the glass, he called to his wife.

"Wife, bring me the Silver Space Spider that spins the purple web."

The Demon Drago's wife left and soon came back with a large silver spider in her hand and set it down on the table.

"Spin," growled the Demon Drago, and the Silver Space Spider began to spin the prettiest purple web the amazed Marzona had ever seen! It was the <u>only</u> purple web she had ever seen. The Silver Space Spider spun the web until it covered the whole table.

When it stopped, the Demon Drago grabbed a piece of the web and put it over a cut on his huge, scraggly right hand. Marzona was surprised to see the cut begin to close! It closed slowly but surely, and soon it was completely gone.

Marzona guessed that the purple web had some special medicine in it. Maybe it would cure her father!

After a while, the Demon Drago lay down on the small sofa and clicked on the TV with a remote control. His wife got up to leave, saying she was going to the kitchen to cook dinner.

Soon the Demon Drago was asleep. Marzona had been waiting for a chance to escape. She quietly eased the closet door open and stepped out. Tiptoeing over to the table, she grabbed the surprised Silver Space Spider.

As fast as her little legs would carry her, Marzona ran until she was out of the door. She soon heard the voice of the Demon Drago yelling for her to stop. She looked back, and saw that he was chasing her, gaining on her fast with his huge feet! She ran and ran and ran.

She didn't stop until she was at the Magic Ladder.

It was much harder climbing up the ladder than it had been climbing down, and many times Marzona wanted to stop and rest, but the Demon Drago was climbing up fast behind her. As soon as Marzona was back in her yard, she picked up the Magic Coin, the ladder disappeared, and the hole closed. The Magic Coin was the only thing left. She picked it up and ran as fast as she could into the house.

Marzona’s parents were getting worried and were very happy to see her, even her sick father managed to smile. Marzona told them about the Demon Drago's palace. Then she showed them the Silver Space Spider. Her mother didn’t believe that a Silver Space Spider could spin a purple web, and even if it could, she didn’t think that a purple web could help Marzona’s father.

“Spin!” Marzona told the spider and almost immediately the Silver Space Spider covered the table with a purple web. Marzona took a piece of the web and placed it on her father’s head. In no time at all, he was up and smiling, looking like he had never been sick!

“See, I told you that coin was magic.”

Marzona and her parents were so happy that they all kissed and hugged each other and danced around the room. But even though Marzona’s father was okay, they still had no money or food.

Marzona knew that only part of her wish had come true, and she guessed that there was something else at the Demon Drago's palace that would make her whole dream come true.

She had to go back.

Early the next morning, Marzona got up before the sun came up, and went outside. She placed the Magic Coin on the ground, watched the coin glow, saw the hole open, and once again climbed down the Magic Ladder until she reached the bottom.

As before, she walked up the golden hill to the Demon Drago's palace. When his wife opened the door, she screamed.

"Go away, go away. You are the girl that took the Silver Space Spider that spins the purple web."

"I meant no harm," Marzona explained. "My father was sick, and I had to do it to make him better. I promise I will bring it back. My father is well now."

"Well, isn't that nice. You are a very good little girl to take such chances to make your father better. Your parents should be very proud of you." The Demon Drago's wife smiled. "Come on in and have a cool drink, and then you can go home and bring back the Silver Space Spider that spins the purple web."

As soon as Marzona sat down, she heard the big feet of the Demon Drago coming, and she ran to hide in the closet!

"Like grass in the springtime and flowers in bloom, the air is filled with a little girl's perfume. Bring her to me; I will have her I will. I want to make her my morning meal!" he shouted.

"There is no little girl here," said his wife. "Come and relax and have something cool to drink."

Once again, the Demon Drago gulped down his drink

and ate his glass with mighty chews.

"Bring me the Midasian Mite," he ordered his wife as he lay down on the sofa.

For the first time, Marzona saw that there was a golden cage hanging in the corner of the room and inside that cage was a little man, barely six inches tall. The Demon Drago's wife took the little man out and placed him on the table. Then the Demon Drago put a coat button on the table next to the little man.

"Touch!" the Demon Drago roared, and the Midasian Mite touched the button, which immediately turned to gold! Then the Demon Drago placed several other things on the table; a glass, a dish and a spoon, and told the Midasian Mite to touch them, and they too turned to gold.

Soon the Demon Drago picked up the Midasian Mite and put him back in his little cage and went to the kitchen. Marzona guessed Midasian Mites could turn anything to gold, except people. She knew that the Midasian Mite was the other part of her wish. For a while, she waited until she was sure the Demon Drago wasn't coming right back.

Then she crept carefully out of the closet and went over to the golden cage and opened the door.

The Midasian Mite was very surprised to see Marzona but so happy to be freed from the cage that he hugged Marzona and kissed her cheek, saying "bless you," over and over again.

He was so loud that the Demon Drago heard the noise and came stomping out of the kitchen just as Marzona was running out the door. He took off after them. The little girl ran as fast as she could, but the Demon Drago was getting closer!

Marzona put the Midasian Mite in her pocket and was soon down the golden hill, had reached the end and was at the bottom of the Magic Ladder. Once again, she climbed up the Magic Ladder as fast as she could. When she looked back, she saw that the Demon Drago was climbing the ladder too, but this time he was coming up even faster!

She began to scream and shriek and climb much faster. She could hear the Demon Drago below her also climbing faster.

It seemed like forever, but soon, she was outside the hole; however the Demon Drago was still coming! He got closer and closer to the top, and as she came out of the hole, he nearly grabbed her foot. She quickly picked up the Magic Coin off the ground.

As soon as the Magic Coin was in her hand, the hole and ladder were gone. Marzona was safe.

Later, Marzona told her parents about her second trip to the palace of the Demon Drago and showed them the Midasian Mite. The Midasian Mite was so grateful to be free that he turned all the trees in Marzona's yard solid gold!

With so much gold, they would be rich and never have to worry about money again.

Marzona and her parents soon let the Midasian Mite go back to his planet and gave the Silver Space Spider that spins the purple web to the King to make medicine for all the people on the planet.

When there was enough medicine she kept her promise and returned the Silver Space Spider to the Demon Drago's wife.

That was the last time she used the Magic Coin and she, her mother and her father faced a joyful future together.

PROTON, THE SHRINKING ROBOT

On a planet in a far off galaxy lives an old robot technician. He lives in an old spaceship that cannot fly, with his pet mechano-monkey, Max, and his two furry Silver Space Spiders; Sam and Sim.

The old technician's name is Rivon and he works for the planet's King, repairing robots. Robots are used by everyone and the King has the biggest and fastest robots on the planet.

Rivon has no robot of his own though.

The King doesn't want him to have one because he wants Rivon to spend his time repairing the kingdom's robots. He doesn't want that time being spent talking to personal robots.

Rivon is not happy.

He wants his own robot. He wants a friend he can talk to and share secrets with. But what could he do? The King had forbid him to buy a robot and would not give Rivon one of his own.

One day Rivon had an idea. If he couldn't buy a robot or get one of the King's as his own he could make his own robot.

What a brilliant idea! He had many parts in the little shop inside his spaceship. He was sure he had enough for a whole robot!

The next day Rivon went to work with a smile on his face. He worked hard all day as the King's Robot Guards brought many robots in that needed fixing. He fixed them as fast as he could and sent them back to the King's palace, but his heart was not in his work. He wanted to begin creating his own robot.

As night came, Rivon fixed his last robot of the day. Gleeful and eager, he began taking the parts and putting together his own robot. Rivon used parts from all kinds of robots and built his own - legs from this model, arms from that one, ears from another, and eyes from one more. It was shabby-looking, but not to Rivon.

"You're beautiful!" said Rivon. "Now I have someone to talk to and keep me company."

Max the mechano-monkey looked angry. He didn't like Rivon forgetting him. Rivon could talk to him but he couldn't talk back.

Then Rivon realized he still had one problem. Power cells were the batteries that made all robots go and Rivon had none. They were all owned by the

King and no one on the planet could have any unless they got them from the King.

What was Rivon to do? If he tried to get power cells from the King, the King would know Rivon had his own robot. There would be no way he could keep his robot secret. The King did not allow robot mechanics to own power cells.

“Oh, I do wish I had power cells for my beautiful robot,” Rivon cried. “I have to find a way to make you work! I need someone to talk to.”

“Well,” said Rivon. Until I get some power cells, I can't talk to you because you can’t talk back! But, at least I have you now. What shall I call you?”

Rivon thought about it for awhile. “Proton! That's it! I’ll call you Proton. Oh Proton, I wish you could talk to me!”

Again, Rivon became sad.

A Mysterious Maiden from Mars heard Rivon’s wishes as she was flying by the planet. She decided she would grant Rivon's wish. She went home to her own planet saying to herself she would return the next day.

All the next day Rivon repaired the King’s robots. His mind was not on his work for all he could think about was finding some power cells for his robot friend, Proton. Many times he thought about stealing the power cells from the King's robots he was repairing, but he knew stealing was wrong. So all day he worked on, until nightfall came.

That night, when everyone was sleeping, the Mysterious Maiden from Mars returned and came to Rivon’s spaceship. From her magic bag she removed a pure power cell and placed it inside of Proton’s chest.

Immediately, Proton came to life! He opened his eyes and stood up. Max the mechano-monkey was awakened and began to squeal, pointing at Proton and hopping up and down.

Before the Mysterious Maiden from Mars left, she decided to give Rivon someone else to talk to. She then blew a kiss at Max and he began to yell, "look, look, Rivon, he's alive, he's alive!"

The loud noise woke up Rivon. He could not believe his ears. Max the mechano-monkey was talking! But he was even more surprised to see his robot friend Proton standing over him moving and smiling and saying, "hello."

The old technician was so happy he jumped out of bed.

"Whoopee!" he yelled. "Now I have two friends to talk to!"

Proton did not know what was going on and neither did Max but they were happy that Rivon was happy.

"Lets all sit around the table, have a family meal, with milk and cookies, and talk," said Rivon. "We are a real family now. I'm so happy everybody can talk to each other. We'll all sit down, eat dinner, and have some milk and cookies together. There is nothing I like better than a family dinner, with milk and cookies, and talking to friends."

However, Rivon had forgotten. He had no milk and cookies. It had been so long since he had a friend to talk to he had not bought any.

"I will go out and buy milk and cookies," said Proton.

"That's a good idea," said Rivon. "You go and buy the milk and cookies."

And he gave Proton some money.

Max wasn't so sure it was a good idea. "I'll go with him Rivon, he may get lost."

Rivon laughed. "He can't get lost. He is programmed to know the way. But you go with him anyway. When you come back we can eat dinner, and get to bond as a family should before we have the milk and cookies."

Proton took Rivon's skycle and Max jumped on behind. They flew over Rivon's space car on their way to the city. When they got there, Proton smiled happily. He was glad to be alive. He waved at everybody he saw and they waved back. Proton was having a great time being out in the city with his new friend Max.

Large and small spaceships flew overhead and Proton waved to them too, enjoying his trip down to the fast moving sidewalk.

A girl named Lazerina was also out by herself. She was not a good girl. She told stories that were not true, she stole things and she even talked mean to her mommy and daddy. When Lazerina saw Proton and Max she said, “Hum, I wonder if that dumb-looking robot has any money.”

“Hi handsome,” said Lazerina. “What do you have in your hand?”

“Money,” said Proton. “I’m going to buy milk and cookies.”

You should buy ice cream instead,” said Lazerina. “I like ice cream.”

“No Proton,” said Max. “Rivon has his heart set on milk and cookies. Besides, this girl wants to eat all the ice cream she’s telling you to buy. If you buy ice cream, Rivon won't have anything!”

Proton paid no attention. He followed Lazerina to

the ice cream parlor.

"Where did you get so much money?" asked the man in the ice cream parlor.

"My friend Rivon gave it to me," said Proton.

"To buy ice cream?" the man questioned.

"Yes, to buy ice cream, a gallon."

This was a lie.

As soon as Proton finished saying it, he started shrinking!

"What's happening to you?" said Max. Proton shrunk one full foot and then stopped shrinking.

Proton took the ice cream and went out of the store as fast as he could. Lazerina and Max followed close behind.

"Let me hold the ice cream for you," said Lazerina, "and we'll all walk somewhere together and sit down to have a little. And, of course we'll save some for your good old friend and mine, Rivon."

Proton gave Lazerina the gallon of ice cream. Max shook his head and the three of them continued down the moving sidewalk.

Lazerina was behind Proton and Max and as they moved on their way she slipped open the ice cream and began to eat it.

She was such a fast eater that the gallon of ice cream was gone in almost no time I all. When she was finished, she slipped into a store without Proton and Max seeing her. They were busy arguing about buying the ice cream.

When the two of them looked back, she was gone.

"You see!" shouted Max. "I warned you. Now Rivon will have no milk and cookies and no ice cream either. You don't have enough money to buy milk and cookies, anymore."

“I have enough money,” Proton said.

Again, Proton was lying.

As soon as he did, he shrunk another foot!

“You do not have enough money!” said Max. “You used too much when you bought the gallon of ice cream. You should not have bought it.”

“I have my own life. I can make my own decisions,” said Proton.

“That does not mean you should decide to lie,” said Max. “At least you have enough money left to get some milk or some cookies. You can’t afford both. So you must use what you have left to buy one or the other. I think you should buy the milk. We have some cake back at Rivon’s spaceship. We can still sit around the table after dinner and talk, but instead of milk and cookies we’ll just have milk and cake.”

Proton and Max stopped at the store and bought

some milk. They went back to where they left the skycle and flew off to Rivon's spaceship. As they flew away from the busy city, four Sneaky Strangers followed them. They were known by most people as the Rip-Off Riders.

"I sure do like milk," said one of the strangers.

"So do we," said the others, as they all laughed, staying close behind Proton and Max.

"I've got an idea," said the leader. "Come on."

The Rip-Off Riders flew their skycles faster until they caught up with Proton and Max.

"Hello friend," said the leader. "You are sure one strong-looking robot. Why I bet you could be one of the King's robots if you wanted to. How would you like to meet the King?"

"The King? Oh yes, I sure would," said Proton, slowing his skycle to a stop. "What do I have to do?"

"I have a King's Castle Credit Card," said the leader. "He asked me to be on the lookout for fine strong robots like you to be members of his Palace Guard. He said if I saw any to give them this credit card. But I was told to get something from the robots I send in return for the credit card. What do you have?"

"I don't have anything," said Proton. "I had some money but most of it is gone."

"Tell you what," said the leader of the Rip-Off Riders, "because I like your strong looks and just because I'm a nice guy, I'll give you this credit card if you give me your milk. That is your milk, right?"

"Of course it is," said Proton.

Another lie!

Proton shrunk another foot, but he didn't care, he ad a credit card to see the King!

The Rip-Off Riders flew off and Proton changed

course to head for the King's palace. He ignored Max begging him to turn back and go home.

When they got to the palace, the first thing they saw was the King's Robot Guard. There were hundreds of robots lined up in rows so many it would take a lifetime to count them all. Behind them stood the King's palace, so large it was bigger than the city they had just left.

"You'd better stop telling lies," said Max. "Look at you. You're almost as small as me now."

A voice yelled up to them. "I am the Keeper of the King's Gate. What do you want?"

They both looked down and saw that the voice was coming from a woman in black uniform, with a chest full of medals.

Proton lowered the skycle. He gave the woman the credit card.

"What is this?" said the woman, looking at the

card. “Oh, I see, another so-called credit card,” she laughed. “The Rip-Off Riders fooled another one! Look robot, I don’t know what they told you but this card will not get you in to see the King.”

“But, they said the King was looking for robots to join his Palace Guard.”

“I’m sorry robot,” said the Gate Keeper, “but all the robots in the King’s Palace Guard are made only for the King. The King would never have a robot like you in his Robot Guard. You're too small and you look like someone threw you together in a junk yard! You have to leave!”

Proton looked sadly at Max. He had no money, no ice cream, no milk, no cookies and he was almost half the size he was when they left Rivon’s spaceship.

As he guided the skycle away from the King's palace, he began to cry.

On the way back, Proton decided to take a short cut over the Robot Recycling Yards where all the old robots were crushed to be recycled into new ones.

Max didn't want Proton to fly over the Robot Recycling Yards. He told Proton that it was against the King's rules.

But again, Proton wouldn't listen. Flying over the Robot Recycling Yards, they saw many different colored cubes stacked as high as they were flying. They flew over some and between others.

In a room deep below the Robot Recycling Yards, a man was watching the two of them on a flat screen video monitor.

He was Evil Ion, the bionic Robot Recycler. He was in charge of the Robot Recycling Yards.

"What have we here," said Evil Ion, "a robot and a mechano-monkey flying over my Recycling Yards? Who do they think they are-the King? Well, I'll show them. I'll recycle that little robot into a bite-size cube and I'll make that little mechano-monkey my slave."

Then Evil Ion reached over and pushed a button. The skycle was soon caught in a tractor beam! It stopped in mid-air and began to go straight down.

Proton tried to fly away but could do nothing to stop the skycle from being pulled out of the sky.

"What's happening?" Max said. "See I told you not to go this way. We're being pulled down by a tractor beam! We're in big trouble."

When the skycle landed on the ground, they faced Evil Ion.

"What are you two fools doing flying over my Robot Recycling Yards? Don't you know it is forbidden?"

"No sir we did not know," said Proton, shrinking

another foot. “If we had known, we would have never done it.” He shrank a little more.

“Why didn’t you know?” said Evil Ion, standing tall over them. “Are you new to this planet? Do you not know the rules?”

“No sir, we did not know,” said Proton. “I am new on this planet and I have only been alive for a little while. I have much to learn.”

“Ha, ha, ha,” laughed Evil Ion. “Yes, you do have a lot to learn.” But surely, you knew flying over the Yards was against the rules even if you only came to life last night.”

“No, I didn’t. said Proton, “Ask my friend Max".

“What is this you say?” said Evil Ion. “You expect me to talk to a mechano-monkey? Mechano-monkeys are not programmed to talk! Do you take me to be a fool?”

"No sir. He can talk, believe me. We didn't know it was wrong to fly over the Robot Recycling Yards."

"You know something, you lying robot. You had better be glad that mechano-monkey can't talk because he would have told you that. Even a mechano-monkey knows better than to fly over Evil Ion's Robot Recycling Yards. Besides, if he could talk, he would have told you not to fly over here in the first place! Isn't that right little mechano-monkey?" Evil Ion laughed. He expected no answer and received none. Max was too scared to say anything.

"Say something Max," said Proton. "Make him believe me. I always tell the truth."

Proton shrank even more!

He was now only one foot tall.

"What is this," laughed Evil Ion, "a shrinking robot? I'd better hurry up and put you in the recycler before you shrink away to nothing."

Then Proton pinched Max. “Ouch,” he said.

Evil Ion was amazed. “So you can talk, huh? Hmmm, you may be more valuable then I thought. I bet people will pay a lot of money to come see my talking mechano-monkey.”

He reached his big hands down and grabbed Proton and Max by the backs of the neck and picked them up.

“I’m taking you, talking mechano-monkey and putting you in a cage, and you,” he said to Proton, “I am going to put you into the recycler before you shrink away! But before I do I want to know why you are shrinking.”

“I don’t know.” Proton lied again, and again he shrank.

He started out at six feet tall and was now only six inches tall!

“He shrinks when he lies,” said Max.

“Ha, ha, that’s hilarious,” laughed Evil Ion. “You must be powered with pure power cells. You can’t even get them on this planet. You must have gotten them from one of those Mysterious Maidens from Mars who go around the galaxy granting wishes.

“I don't know,” said the now tiny Proton. “All I know is that I’m here. I don't know how I got here or why. I don't know why everything I do seems to turn out wrong.”

“You see shrinking robot, those pure power cells in you run on good energy. That means that when you tell the truth and do good things you will grow and be strong and people will love you. And above all, you won’t get yourself into the kind of trouble you’re in now,” Evil Ion growled. “But, you deserve to be in trouble because you had pure power cells in you, the best in the universe, if you are good; but you, you mini-robot were bad, bad, bad! You'll never get a chance to use that power inside of you to grow strong because in your short life you did not learn that life was given to you to be good and to do good. So I must recycle you now bad little shrinking robot. If I wait any longer you will be so small you won't fit on my little finger."

Evil Ion carried Proton and Max over to a very large and scary machine. Robots and pieces of robots lay on a moving belt, each disappearing into a hole followed by crunching noises. This machine was the recycler.

"Stay here my little talking mechano-monkey, while I recycle your pocket-sized robot friend," said Evil Ion as he put mechano-monkey down.

Just then purple rain began falling from the sky.

"Well my little pinky ring, it looks like you get to

see some beautiful purple rain on your first and last day alive." Evil Ion placed Proton on the moving belt and he Proton moving toward the hole in the front of the recycler.

"No! No!," Proton begged. "Please don't recycle me sir! I'll be good. I promise I will. I'll promise to use the good inside of me. I will stop lying and will be good to people and do what's right. Please! Please!"

"Sorry, you bad shrinking robot. It's too late. Life is short. You have to learn fast!"

Just as Proton reached the opening of the recycler the belt came to a screeching stop. Evil Ion cussed the purple rain for messing up his fun.

"Stay there little bad shrinking robot. I will be with you in a second. This machine always breaks down when the purple rain falls. Funny, it doesn't do that with any other color. Anyway, it'll only take a second to fix it."

While Evil Ion was busy pushing different buttons on his electronic keypad, trying to reboot the recycler, Max had slipped away, and flew off on Rivon's skycle.

As fast as he could, he flew to Rivon's spaceship.

"Rivon!" he yelled. "Proton is in trouble. Evil Ion the bionic Robot Recycler is about to recycle him into a pinky ring."

"My poor robot friend. Let's hurry and save him. Come we'll take my space car."

Rivon ran outside and jumped into the space car with Max close behind. The space car was up and off in a split second flying like a bright orange blur!

Soon they were landing in the Robot Recycling Yards right next to the recycler where Proton still lay on the belt. Evil Ion was nowhere around.

Rivon picked Proton up from the belt.

"What happened to you Proton? Why are you so

small now?"

But, Proton had no time to answer for Evil Ion came running from his house with a very large wrench. "Stop!" he shouted. "That's my new pinky ring you're taking there."

"Run, Proton!" yelled Rivon.

Proton ran. Max ran.

Rivon ran too.

But they could not get back to Rivon's space car. Evil Ion was in their way. So they ran in between the many colored stacks of metal cubes trying to get away.

Evil Ion was gaining on Rivon as the old man slowed more and more, too tired to go on.

Then Rivon felt a hand on his shoulder! He was caught by Evil Ion, but was glad that Proton and Max had gotten away.

"So, old man you are foolish enough to try and

come here at my Robot Recycling Yards and attempt a rescue. You are as dumb as your miniature robot friend. And since I can't recycle him, I'll recycle you."

Evil Ion picked Rivon up over his head and carried him like a piece of paper over to the recycler. Then he strapped Rivon onto the belt.

"Well now I can use this wrench to make a few minor adjustments, and the recycler will have some dinner after all-YOU!" Evil Ion snarled at the very scared old man.

With a few turns of Evil Ion's wrench and a few more taps on his keypad, the machine began to hum and the belt began to move. Rivon came closer, closer, closer, closer, closer...

Suddenly, the sky was filled with skycles; hundreds, maybe thousands. Evil Ion knew it could only mean one thing-the King!

Sure enough it was the King and he came down from the sky on his skycle.

"What's going on here?" The King demanded to know. "Ion, are you crushing people now? I don't pay you to recycle people, just robots."

"Yes, my King, I know," said Evil Ion, shyly. "I wasn't really going to crush the old man. I was, uh, just trying to scare him a little. He broke the rules. He flew over here without your permission."

"Well, this little robot says you were going to crush the old man," the King said.

"That little robot is a liar," said Evil Ion. "Look at him. You can tell. That's why he keeps shrinking.

"That's not true!" shouted Proton.

With that lie, Proton now was barely visible. It was true. He was getting smaller because he kept telling lies.

“What would you know about the truth, little worthless shrinking robot?” said Evil Ion. “Look at him King, he's so small you can barely see him. He's powered with pure power cells.”

“That's impossible.” the King said. “No one on this planet has pure power cells to put in their robots except me, unless he got them from the Mysterious Maidens from Mars.”

“He must have,” said Evil Ion, “but he claims he doesn't know.”

“Hmmm,” the King said. “Maybe this is a bad robot. How long did it take you to get this small robot?

“One day,” said Proton.

“Only one day? You did a lot of lying today then. Maybe Ion is right, Maybe you need to go into the recycler. You are a robot who has learned nothing in this short life. Ion, let the old man go. Proceed with recycling this lying little robot."

Proton couldn't believe what he was hearing. He tried to run but there was nowhere to go. The King's Robot Guards were everywhere.

"No! Please! Don't!" Rivon begged the King. "Don't recycle my friend. He's all that I have. I only made him because I was lonely. I wished he had power cells because I didn't have any. A Mysterious Maiden from Mars must have heard me and gave him pure power cells. I didn't know! If I knew, I would have warned him that his life was given to him only that he may do good!"

The King looked at Rivon, who was on his knees begging and pleading. He saw how much Proton meant to the old man. He could never break up such a friendship by recycling the little robot.

"Rivon," he said. "Your love for this robot has touched my heart. I will give him another chance at life. I will not have him recycled."

"Oh thank you great one," sobbed Rivon.

"As for you my little friend," the King said to Proton. "I'm giving you another chance. Make the best of it. Remember life is to be used for good. It is the only way to live. You must learn that. You must *live* that. You did not learn it today and see what almost happened to you. The choice is yours. You can lie and die or be good and live. Now go, all of you before I change my mind."

Rivon, Proton and Max put the skycle in back of the space car and were soon at Rivon's spaceship. Rivon looked at the inch-high Proton. "You must have done a lot of bad things in one day to get this small Proton." he said. "What happened?"

"Remember to tell the truth." said Max.

Proton told Rivon about everything just the way it happened. As he talked he grew and grew and grew until he was his just as tall as Rivon again.

"Never again," Proton sighed, "will I do anything bad or tell another lie. Lying makes you small and weak, the truth makes you big and strong"

THE WAY-OUT WIZARD OF THE WESTERN STAR

On planet in a far off galaxy the people had a problem: Space Snakes!

The planet was overrun with them. Long, short, fat and thin. They attacked people's pets and ended up in many beds at night. But they didn't wait until night to come out. They roamed the cities of the planet in the daytime, coming and going as they pleased. Everyday there were more and more of them and the sound of hissing could be heard day and night.

The people of the planet had tried everything they could think of but nothing seemed to do any good.

The people of the planet became very angry. They stood outside the King's palace and demanded that something be done about those terrible Space Snakes.

The King knew he had to do something. He did not want his people to get so mad that they would be looking for a new King. He called together his advisors.

"What should I do about this problem we are having with these Space Snakes?" He asked.

"I think we should leave and let the Space Snakes have the planet," said one.

"I think we should try stronger poison," said another.

"I think we should give all the people baseball bats," said still another.

The King thought about what his advisors said. "Well, we cannot leave the planet to the Space Snakes. We have no other planet to go to and I would rather be King of a Space Snake planet than King of no planet at all. We've already tried the strongest poison made and using baseball bats would take forever. We need to do something now," he said. "No, these ideas are no good. We need to do something else. I will send a subspace message to all the other planets offering a reward to anyone who comes up with an idea that will work."

So the King sent a message throughout the galaxy that he would give one million creditrons to whoever could rid his planet of the Space Snakes.

Soon people were coming from all over the galaxy and even through wormholes from other galaxies, to try and win the reward.

People came with new traps, new poisons, even other animals to eat the Space Snakes, but nothing at all worked.

Weeks passed and the steady flood of people with ideas did little to stop the Space Snakes that were now so many that the city streets looked like one giant wiggling Space

Snake!

One evening the King was listening to a man who had an idea to freeze the planet and when the Space Snakes died to thaw it out again, but he couldn't explain how the people would keep from freezing too.

As the King was sending the man on his way, another man came in. He was very short and quiet-looking. He was dressed in a purple mask, a purple robe and a purple derby hat. On his left eye was a purple eye-patch and around his neck hung a square purple mirror. As he walked to the King, he seemed to float as if walking on air.

"I am the Way-Out Wizard of the Western Star," said the little man. "I am here to collect my reward."

"First, you have to get rid of the Space Snakes," said the King.

"I will get rid of the Space Snakes," said the Way-Out Wizard of the Western Star, but you must promise me on your honor as a good person and a King to pay me one million creditrons."

"I promise," said the King. "Upon my honor as a good person and a King, I will pay you one million creditrons if you get rid of these Space Snakes."

The Way-Out Wizard of the Western Star went outside and placed the square purple mirror he was wearing around his neck on the ground. Soon the mirror began to grow and grow and grow and it began to make the same sound that Space Snakes were making - hissssssssss!

Space Snakes came from everywhere; every city on the planet. Young Space Snakes, old Space Snakes, big Space Snakes, small Space Snakes, long Space Snakes, short Space Snakes, Space Snakes of all colors and kinds. And, as the purple mirror hissed the space snakes came to it, one-by-one disappearing into the mirror.

All day Space Snakes came and all night as each and every

one of them disappeared into the square purple mirror. The people of the planet could not believe their eyes! What was this magic purple mirror that this strange little Wizard had? How did it work?

They were so happy to see the Space Snakes disappearing they really didn't care how it was done. Finally, as a new day came the last of the Space Snakes disappeared into the square purple mirror.

When the Way-Out Wizard of the Western Star was satisfied that all the Space Snakes were gone he hung the square purple mirror around his neck and went back to see the King.

The King had decided to break his promise to pay the Wizard.

"The Space Snakes are gone now," said the King, "and I will not pay you a million creditrons. I will only give you a half-million."

"But you promised." said the Way-Out Wizard of the Western Star. "You should never break a promise because if you do bad things will happen to you."

The King only laughed at the Way-Out Wizard of the Western Star and gave him a half-million creditrons instead of the one million he had promised.

The Way-Out Wizard of the Western Star shook his head and he turned to leave. When he reached the door he turned around again.

"I'm giving you one last chance," he said to the laughing King. "You do not understand that you should never break a promise."

Still, the King just laughed.

The Way-Out Wizard of the Western Star floated out the door and went back outside to the place where the Space Snakes had disappeared into the square purple mirror. He once again removed the purple mirror from around his neck and placed it on the ground.

"Laugh and laugh foolish King, laugh 'til the end of time, for soon you will learn that breaking a promise is a laughing crime. You can laugh all you want, loud and clear, for soon no more laughter will you hear." he said.

Soon the purple mirror began to grow again and the sound coming from it sounded like children laughing. The sound got louder and louder and louder. The King and his advisors came to see what the noise was. Other people came too. Why had the Way-Out Wizard of the Western Star placed his mirror on the street again they all asked each other.

Then groups of children started to come from the buildings laughing and playing, sounding just like the sound coming from the purple mirror! Then they began walking to and disappearing into the purple mirror just as the Space Snakes had done!

The King and his advisors and the other people tried to stop the Way-Out Wizard of the Western Star but found out that there feet were stuck to the ground, and their voices did not work.

So, all they could do was stand there. They stood there like statues and watched all of the children of the planet come and disappear into the Way-Out Wizard of the Western Star's mirror one by one.

When the last child on the planet had disappeared into the Way-Out Wizard of the Western Star's square purple mirror it shrank to the size it was before and he picked it up and placed it around his neck. He then took off his purple derby, putting it on the ground.

Then he floated up into the sky and was gone.

There was not one child left on the planet!

From that day on no more children were born there. It was a very sad place because without the laughter of children everyone on the planet soon forgot how to laugh. And, to this day the Way-Out Wizard of the Western Star's purple derby is still there as a reminder to the people of the planet never to break a promise.

On it were written the last words the Wizard had said:

"Laugh and laugh foolish King. Laugh 'til the end of time. Soon you will learn that breaking a promise is a laughing crime. You can laugh all you want, loud and clear for soon no more laughter will you hear."

WONDERINA'S WORLD OF SURPRISES

In a far off galaxy there is a little girl named Wonderina who loves to have fun. She will play all day long and all night too, if her parents let her. She never gets tired of playing. Everyday, she would play all the games she had learned from mommy and daddy. She would also play the games she learned in school from her teachers and class mates. Once she was done, she would make up new games.

“I wish I could be a Space Pirate,” said Wonderina one day while she was playing. “Everything is so boring and I want to do something new and interesting.”

“Yes,” said her friend Gan-Dor. “Let’s do something we have never done before.”

It was summertime. School had just closed for summer vacation. Wonderina and Gan-Dor loved to go to school and didn’t like being out of school for a whole Summer.

“We can’t really be Space Pirates,” said Gan-Dor, "because we would go to jail.”

“I know that,” said Wonderina, “but can’t we think of something?”

“Let’s think about it.”

So they thought and thought and thought. Neither of them said anything while they thought. Then Wonderina slowly cleared her throat.

"Hmmm... I know, she said. "Let's become a Cosmic Corporation!"

"What's a Corporation?" questioned Gan-Dor.

"Oh, it's just a fancy word for business. You know like a candy store, only bigger."

"Oh," said Gan-Dor. "But why don't we just become a big business or a big candy store?"

"Because silly, a Cosmic Corporation doesn't have to pay a lot of taxes so it makes more money than a regular business or a candy store."

Wonderina really didn't know what taxes were. She remembered hearing her daddy say something about them being too high a few times. She hoped Gan-Dor wouldn't ask her what taxes were.

He didn't, so she kept talking.

"We'll call ourselves the Space-age Surprise Cosmic Corporation. I'll be the President, and you can be the Vice-

President.”

“All right,” said Gan-Dor, willing to do anything his friend suggested. “But what are we going to do with our Cosmic Corporation? Sell candy? I would like that!”

“No we're not going to sell candy. We're going to give people surprises.”

“What kind of Cosmic Corporation gives surprises?” Gan-Dor said.

“Our kind. It’s ours’ isn’t it? So we can do anything we want to do. No one said our Cosmic Corporation had to be the same as everybody else’s. Besides my parents always tell me it’s better to give that to receive.”

“What kind of surprises will we give?” Gan-Dor wanted to know.

“Only good surprises,” said Wonderina. “I would never give a bad surprise. We’ll find people who need things done for them and we will do them. But, we won’t tell them who did it and make them wonder how the things happened. I know we'll get a lot of fun out of it."

"I think the same thing." said Gan-Dor.

"Okay, I'll make a list of things and then we'll decide which to do first."

Wonderina went over and sat down in front of the iPad computer her parents had given her for her birthday. She tapped on the touchscreen and a list began to appear.

"Now remember, we are going to surprise people so we have to keep our Cosmic Corporation a secret. So don't tell anybody," she said quietly, as she touched the "save" key and the monitor screen went blank.

"You don't have to tell me that. What do you think I am dumb or something?" replied Gan-Dor.

Later that afternoon, Wonderina's mother returned from work in her space car. She was tired and thirsty from the heat of the summery day. So she went into the kitchen to get something to drink. On the way she remembered those dirty breakfast dishes she still had to wash. When she got there, she couldn't believe her eyes! The kitchen was sparkling clean! There were no dirty breakfast dishes. No dirty anything! Everything was in its place; the table was set for dinner, all the kitchen appliances were shining, the floor had been mopped, and even the windows were clean!

What happened? For a minute she wondered if a Mysterious Maiden from Mars had granted a wish or something.

Wonderina and Gan-Dor came in. Her mother asked whether either of them saw anyone cleaning up in the kitchen.

"No, we didn't see anyone cleaning but it sure looks like they've been busy," Wonderina laughed.

Wonderina's mother leaned back in her chair and

sipped a cold drink. “Well,” it’s just perfect. I have no more work to do today and now I can relax and watch a movie on satellite TV. I wonder who did it all. You two are too busy playing to clean-up and your father is away on a business trip...”

Then she opened a letter she had found on the floor when she came in. It read:

“The Space-age Surprise Cosmic Corporation was here this afternoon on a little matter of business.”

“I wonder what that means,” Mother asked.

“I wonder,” smiled Wonderina.

“Can I stay for dinner?” Gan-Dor asked Wonderina’s mother. “I’ve already texted my mom and she says its okay.”

“Of course you can,” she replied. “You know you are always welcome in our house.”

So the three of them sat down and ate dinner.

The next morning old Mr. Jon-zen, who lived down the street, walked outside and found a basket of food on his doorstep.

"Who could have done this?" he wondered. "Where did all this delicious-looking food come from?"

Looking at a card left with the food he read, "With love from the Space-age Surprise Cosmic Corporation."

Morox Marex, a school friend of Wonderina and Gan-Dor was at home with a broken leg.

The doctor told him he had to stay off his feet or the leg would hurt more. He was very sad because he couldn't go outside and play and he had nothing to do inside. All he could do was sit in the bed and look out the window.

One day a toy remote-controlled purple plane flew through his window, buzzing as it circled the room. On top of it was a long box that seemed too heavy for the tiny plane. The purple plane circled Morox's bed and stopped and turned sideways dropping the box on Morox's lap. Then it flew back out of the window and disappeared.

Morox opened the box. New books! Just what he's been longing for! He loved to read and had read all the old books in his room.

Every day that Summer the Space-age Surprise Cosmic Corporation surprised someone with a good surprise by doing something nice for them.

One day they decided to leave another basket of food for Mr. Jon-zen. They were so eager to get the food to the old man that they didn't see Wonderina's mother standing across the street watching them. Now she guessed who had been leaving all those nice surprises for the neighbors.

The Space-age Surprise Cosmic Corporation was no longer a secret.

A few days later a letter came to Wonderina's house addressed to the Space-age Surprise Cosmic Corporation inviting the members to a party at the school playground that afternoon.

When they got there, everyone in the neighborhood were there clapping for them and thanking them for the wonderful surprises. But no one would tell them how they knew who the Space-age Surprise Cosmic Corporation was.

They never did find out how their secret was revealed. It remained a wonderful mystery. Wonderina and Gan-Dor were very happy they helped so many people; it made them feel better than anything they ever did before.

They never knew that helping people was a fun game to play.

Soon all the other kids in the neighborhood joined the Space-age Surprise Cosmic Corporation and each day they worked on giving good surprises for the people in the neighborhood and all of them looked forward to the surprise-filled future together.

ASTRON AND THE SECRET SILOS

On a planet in a far off galaxy there lives an adventurous little boy. His name is Astron.

Astron has very nice parents. His parents let him go anywhere he wants to.

Sometimes he will ride his skycle all over the planet, visiting as many places as he can in one day.

One day when Astron came home from a long ride on his skycle he found his mother in the house crying.

"What's the matter mommy?" He asked.

"Oh, Astron, there is such bad news. Our planet is running out of food. As time goes by there will be less and less to eat. Soon we will all starve," answered his mother.

"Don't worry Mommy. We'll just get food from another planet," said Astron.

"We can't," said his mother. "All the other planets in our galaxy are running out of food too."

"What is happening to it?" Astron wanted to know. His mother just wept and gloomily shook her head.

When they got inside Astron sat at the table with both of his parents. They both looked very sad. On the table was a single loaf of bread and three plates. Each of them also had a glass of water.

"This loaf of bread is all we have left," said Astron's father. "It may be the last meal we have as a family. We should be thankful that we have it and share it together because we have each other."

They all looked at each other. Each of their eyes

filled with tears, they knew that each of them would soon die if they had no food to eat.

"Let's all hold hands," said Astron's mother, "and say together, I love you."

So the three of them joined hands and said, "I love you," to each other. Somehow, it made them all feel better.

Then they ate the last loaf of bread.

"Astron," said Astron's father, "I noticed that you have not ridden your skycle in quite a while. I know you have been worried about the food problem but there is nothing you can do. You should enjoy the time we have left. You are so young, too young, to have known the joy of a long life. Go. Ride your skycle."

"But Father," said Astron. "I want to stay here with you and Mother. You might need me."

“Son, we know you love us and want to help,” said his father.

“There is nothing you can do here and besides it would give me great joy to see you ride again. Go out, enjoy being a little boy. Ride your skycle, for me.”

Astron saw that his father really wanted him to ride his skycle and though he didn’t want to, Astron would do it, to make his father happy. So, Astron went outside and got on his skycle. In seconds, he was soaring high above the rooftops. It had been so long he had almost forgotten how good it felt. For the first time in what seemed like forever he smiled and as he circled above ground, he looked down.

His mother and father were smiling too. Then, Astron decided to ride around the planet and do some adventuring. As he flew, he went farther and farther away from the city. He flew and flew and flew. He was having so much fun that he didn't realize that it was getting late.

Soon darkness began to fall and Astron turned around to head back home.

It was a little hard to see the way but the purple moon was full, and Astron guided the skycle by its light.

As he flew over the forest he noticed a clearing in the middle.

There seemed to be people standing down there. So Astron decided to take a closer look. He slowed down his skycle and lowered it into one of the tall trees around the clearing.

There were ten men there standing around another Mean-looking man.

The Mean Man in the Middle of the Men reached down and lifted up a rock. He pulled a round piece of purple glass out from under the rock.

He held the purple glass up in the air.

He stood there like that for a long time. Suddenly, the light of the purple moon came straight down unto the purple glass. Then it went through the purple glass and came out in a purple ray.

The man aimed the purple ray at one of the trees. When the ray hit the tree Astron heard a whirring sound. To his astonishment, the ground was opening up!

The Mean Man in the Middle of the Men kept the purple ray aimed at the tree and soon Astron saw that the opening in the ground was actually two large doors sliding open!

When the man stopped aiming the purple ray at the trees the doors stopped opening.

Astron was curious.

"What is going on here," he wondered. "I sure would like to see what's down there."

Then the ten men followed the man with the glass circle into the hole, down an escalator, and the doors closed behind them.

After waiting a long time Astron was just about to take off on his skycle but the doors started opening, he hid himself in the tree, watching as the men came out.

When they were all out the man with the purple glass circle held it up to the moon again and as soon as the purple ray of light came through the circle and hit the tree the doors began to whirr and close. The man held the purple glass circle there until the doors were completely closed.

When they were closed it looked like there was nothing there but smooth ground. Then the man placed the purple glass circle back under the rock he had gotten it from.

Soon they all boarded their skycles and flew off.

"They looked like horrible men," thought Astron. "I'm glad they didn't see me"

Astron thought about going home but curiosity got the best of him. He just had to see what was in that hole.

So, he guided his skycle down to the ground and went over to the rock, lifted it, and removed the purple glass circle.

He then held the circle up to the moonlight. Just as the man had done. When the purple moon ray came through he guided it to the same tree.

The doors began to open!

Astron's heart was beating very fast. He wanted to know what was down there but he was also very scared.

“What if more men are down there?” he thought.

But he was more curious than scared. He loved adventure, so when the doors were open he went down the escalator, running down as it moved.

Down, down, and down still he rode. Many times he was going to turn around but he just had to see what was down there.

Finally, he reached the end of the escalator and faced a long tunnel, so long! It seemed without end. As he tiptoed down the tunnel he saw that the floor was covered with large circular doors. Each door had a handle on it. Astron bent down and slowly lifted one of the handles and pulled open one of the doors.

“Food!” Meats, breads, fruit, milk, juices, everything anyone could want!

“So this where all the food had been disappearing to. Those men are stealing it!”

Astron decided to get out of there but before he did he filled a bag with all the food he could carry.

Soon he was back outside. He repeated what he saw the man do again and when the door was closed he placed the purple glass circle back under the stone. Then he flew off on his skycle to tell his parents what he had seen.

Astron's parents were amazed at the story. They didn't know what to do. They were worried that the men may come after their adventurous son to take back their food, or even kill him.

Astron's mother decided to hide the food.

"Everyone on the planet knows that we have no food left. If they find out we have it these men may know how we got it," she said.

"You are right," said Astron's father, "and we also have to make the food last a long time, as long as we can. So I think we should check what Astron has brought us and make plans on how much of it we can eat at one time."

They laid the food out on the table and wrote down a list of what they had. Astron had brought a little of everything - meats, breads, fruits, milk and juice, and several other bags, filled with whole grains. They had enough food to last quite a while.

One of the items was a bag of whole wheat grain.

"How much whole wheat grain is this?" said Astron's mother.

"I don't know", said his father. "We'll need a scale to weigh it. We need to know exactly how much it is so that we can make it last as long as we can."

Astron's mother said that they didn't have a digital weighing scale so she would have to borrow one from the people next door.

Na-nine, their next door neighbor, wondered why Astron's mother wanted a scale. "What could they be weighing," she wondered. "I know they don't have any food left."

When the scale was returned Na-nine was very surprised to see a piece of whole wheat grain stuck to the bottom.

"Where did they get whole wheat grain? I thought they had run out of food like everyone else around here. Yet, they have so much grain they need a scale to measure it? It doesn't make sense." Na-nine said to her husband, La-Far. "You have to snoop around over there and find out where they're getting this grain from. Maybe we can get some too."

The next day La-Far watched Astron's house. All day he watched and watched and watched. But neither Astron nor his parents came out. When night fell

Astron came out and got on his skycle. La-Far decided to follow him. He flew his own skycle and stayed behind Astron who led him to the clearing in the woods.

La-Far watched from a tree as Astron removed the purple glass circle from under the rock and guided the purple moonlight ray until the door opened and he stepped inside.

La-Far waited for Astron to come out. When he did he had a large bag over his shoulder. La-Far guessed it must be full of whole grains or other food. Astron again closed the door with the ray of purple moonlight and flew off on his skycle.

La-Far came down from his hiding place and did what he had seen Astron do. Again, the doors open.

"Hurray!" La-Far whispered to himself. He was so excited that he ran down the escalator, dropping the purple glass circle on the ground outside.

The doors closed behind him.

When he got down to the end of the escalator he was filled with greed. He ran here and there pulling open the round doors and filling up bags with all kinds of food. He had so much that he would have to take many trips to get it all out.

When La-Far was ready to leave he carried his bags up the escalator until he got to the closed doors.

They wouldn't open!

He pushed, he pulled, and he pounded. Nothing. Then he remembered.

The purple glass circle!

He had not done everything he saw Astron do. He forgot to take the purple glass circle down with him.

The doors could not open unless he had it. He was trapped!

The next night the men came back to the clearing in the woods.

The leader saw the glass circle next to the doors.

"What is this?" He roared. "How did this get here?"

Then he held the glass circle up and the purple moonlight ray opened the doors again.

Out came La-Far.

"Take him," the Mean Man in the Middle of the Men ordered.

The men then grabbed La-Far and took him away, dropping his hat at the bottom of the escalator steps inside.

"In case there are others who know about our Secret Silos, they will see his hat the next time they come and they will know not to come here again." The Mean Man in the Middle of the Men laughed.

Na-nine was worried. La-Far was still not home and it was now morning. She went to see Astron's parents and told them how she had found out about the whole wheat grain and how La-Far had been sent there to find out where it came from. She also said that she saw him follow Astron on his skycle.

Astron had an idea of what may have happened to La-Far.

That night he went to the clearing and opened the doors to the Silos where all he found was La-Far's hat at the bottom of the escalator. Astron ran out of there as fast as he could! When the doors were closed he jumped on his skycle and then flew home.

He told his parents and Na-nine that all he found was La-Far's hat. All of them were very afraid. But Na-nine wanted Astron to show her where La-Far's hat was. She knew she would never see him again and wanted his hat to remember him by.

"No, No, Na-nine," Astron's father said. "We can't let him go back there. You should not go either. Those evil men may catch you there and do the same thing to you."

They argued and Na-nine moaned. Finally, Astron's father said that Astron could show Na-nine the way.

"Please you two, be careful," he said.

Na-nine climbed on the back of Astron's skycle and off they flew. In no time they were at the clearing. Astron opened the doors as usual. Na-nine went inside and came out with La-Far's hat. Astron closed the doors.

They quickly left as soon as Na-nine climbed on the back of the skycle with La-Far's hat.

Then they flew up and over the trees, speeding

home as fast as they could. Na-nine cried and sobbed all the way there.

She took La-Far's hat home and began calling around to arrange La-Far's memorial service. Soon she had found someone. She took La-Far's hat to the man.

"What happened to him?" the man asked.

"He was taken off by wild animals," answered Na-nine. "And nothing was left, except his hat."

But, the man did not believe her. He guessed she was trying to hide something. So he asked her for a lot more money than usual and she paid it.

"I could keep this accident extra, extra quiet if you want me to," the man said with a cunning smile.

"What do you mean?" said Na-nine.

"I can tell you are trying to hide something," said the man. "But, I will keep your secret if you'd like.

Just give me the rest of your money."

Na-nine gave the man all her money and made him promise not to tell anyone about La-Far.

When Na-nine went home she worried about the man.

Maybe he would tell.

Later that night the Mean Man in the Middle of the Men at the clearing had come to it and opened the doors with the purple moonlight ray.

When he reached the bottom of the escalator he found that La-Far's hat was gone.

"The Secret Silos are no longer secret," he said to his men. "We must find out who else was here and give them the same thing we gave their friend."

The next day the Mean Man in the Middle of the Men went to the city where Astron lived.

The Mean Man in the Middle of the Men knew that

La-Far would have a memorial service soon so he went around to the city's memorial service companies and asked them if they were setting up a memorial service for a man who had disappeared, and only left behind a hat.

Soon he came to the memorial service man Na-nine had gone to. But, the man did not tell. He had kept his word to Na-nine.

Later on, the Mean Man in the Middle of the Men was about to leave the city. As he flew off he passed over a memorial service going on.

He decided to go down and see if he could find out who was being honored. When he landed he left his skycle and went over to the gathering with Na-nine and the others.

Na-nine was crying loudly.

"Why? Why did they have to take my husband

away?"

Now the Mean Man in the Middle of the Men knew who had been in the place of the Secret Silos.

After La-Far's hat was buried he followed Na-nine home. He waited outside until she was alone.

When darkness came the Mean Man in the Middle of the Men went to her door and rang the bell. When she came to answer it he pushed his way inside.

"Okay, old woman," he snarled. "I'm the man who took your husband away. And if you don't want to disappear too you had better tell me who showed you the Secret Silos."

Na-nine's only thought was to protect Astron. Besides, she felt she now had nothing to live for. La-Far was gone.

"I found them," she said.

"You expect me to believe that old woman?" he

shouted. “You are too old to have traveled all that way by yourself. I know someone helped you find the Silos, tell me who it is, or else!”

“No one!” Na-nine said. “If you want to kill me go ahead.”

“I will not kill you yet,” said the Mean Man in the Middle of the Men. “But, I will make you suffer more than losing your husband has made you suffer. By the time I am done you will wish you were dead. You better tell me who helped you find the Secret Silos.”

“Go away!” Na-nine screamed.

Then the door bell rang.

“Answer it,” demanded the Mean Man in the Middle of the Men.

Na-nine went over to the door and opened it.

It was Astron!

Na-nine was so scared all she could blurt out was,

"run!" before she fainted.

Astron ran.

The Mean Man in the Middle of the Men chased him. Astron's young legs carried him much faster than the Mean Man in the Middle of the Men could run and Astron ran inside his parents' house.

He decided not to go after Astron. He would wait. He knew now where to find the one that discovered the Secret Silos. He planned to come back later with his men.

He wanted to be sure he came back to the right house. All the houses looked the same so he marked Astron's door by gently touching his light sword on the door. The small mark it left would show them the right place.

Astron and his parents were huddled together inside scared that the Mean Man in the Middle of the

Men would break in their house and kill them all. They all jumped when they heard the sword touch the door.

Soon after that the Mean Man in the Middle of the Men flew off. Astron and his parents waited a long time after they heard his skycle leave before they stopped hugging each other.

When they calmed down Astron's father looked outside. He didn't see the Mean Man in the Middle of the Men.

"He was so mad he tried to cut a hole in the door." said Astron's father.

"No, a light sword can easily cut a hole in the door. I think he put a mark on our door so he'll know which house to come back to," said Astron's mother.

"Hmmm.... you are probably right Mommy," said Astron.

"Well, when he comes back to town we will make sure he is confused because I will mark a few more doors the same way," Astron's father said.

And, he did.

Very late that night the Mean Man in the Middle of the Men flew back with his mean-looking men. But, when they got there many doors were also marked by a light sword.

The Mean Man in the Middle of the Men did not know which one he made.

Angry, he his mean-looking men returned to the place of the Secret Silos and planned other ways to catch Astron.

The Mean Man in the Middle of the Men told his men to stay at the place of the Secret Silos. He told them of his plan to get into Astron's house.

He was going to dress himself as a food farmer, go

to each house until he found Astron, and fool Astron's parents into letting him in to show them what food he had.

The next day he loaded up the back of his space car with food and flew to Astron's neighborhood, going door-to-door.

When he got to the right house he rang the bell and Astron's father came to the door. Astron was spotted, playing inside.

"I am a farmer," smiled the Mean Man in the Middle of the Men. "I grew some food on my own farm and I am trying to sell it."

Astron's father was so happy to get some food he did not think that it was strange that no one had any food, yet this man had so much that he was selling it.

The Mean Man in the Middle of the Men followed Astron's father inside and put his bags of food on the table. Astron had never really gotten a good look at the Mean Man in the Middle of the Men and did not recognize him at first.

But, Na-nine had been looking out of her window. When she saw the Mean Man in the Middle of the Men go into Astron's house she knew who it was. So she ran to get her laser gun and went over to Astron's house.

When she got there the Mean Man in the Middle of the Men became afraid. He thought Na-nine would tell Astron and his parents who he was.

Na-nine said nothing but kept her laser gun in view and ready.

"I am so lonely and afraid," she told Astron's parents. "Would it be okay if I stayed with you tonight?"

"Sure you can," said Astron's mother. "You can

stay as long as you like."

"Thank you," said Na-nine, pulling out her laser gun and placing it on the table. "I have been so scared that mean man would come back that I didn't sleep last night. I sat up all night long waiting for him with my laser gun. I will do the same thing tonight."

When the Mean Man in the Middle of the Men heard this he quickly got up and left.

He knew that if he tried to get Astron, Na-nine would blast him with her laser gun. When he flew off in his space car, as mad as ever. As soon as he got back to the place of the Secret Silos the Mean Man in the Middle of the Men began working on another idea.

The next day he came back to Astron's house. This time he came dressed as a satellite TV repairman.

"There is nothing wrong with our satellite TV,"

said Astron's mother.

"I know," said the Mean Man in the Middle of the Men, "but I was sent here to check it anyway."

Again, Astron and his parents didn't recognize the Mean Man in the Middle of the Men and they let him in. He was relieved to see that Na-nine was not there. This time he would waste no time.

"Put your hands up," he snarled at Astron and his parents. "I am here to take this boy away and kill him."

Then the Mean Man in the Middle of the Men tied up Astron's parents and dragged the boy outside. He put Astron in the back of his space car.

Just as he was about to fly off Na-nine came running out of her house. She thought the satellite TV repairman looked like the Mean Man in the Middle of the Men and she had been watching.

When the Mean Man in the Middle of the Men saw her coming, he pulled out his laser gun to blast her.

As he aimed Astron jumped up and knocked the laser gun out of his hand and it fell to the ground!

The Mean Man in the Middle of the Men pushed Astron back into his chair and began to guide the space car up into the air.

Na-nine was afraid to shoot. But, she knew that if she didn't Astron would be gone forever!

So she set it to "stun" and fired her laser gun.

Bzzzzzz!

The laser gun blasted and hit the Mean Man in the Middle of the Men's space car right in the back and it began falling to the ground.

He jumped out and ran away.

But he did not get very far.

Na-nine fired another blast and hit him. His clothes

burst into flames as he ran off into the woods screaming.

Astron jumped out of the space car and hugged Na-nine. Then the two of them went inside to untie his parents.

Later on Astron showed the Planet Police how to get into the place of the Secret Silos.

The Mean Man in the Middle of the Men and his mean-looking men were put in jail.

Soon everyone on the planet had all the food they could eat and Astron enjoyed a future filled with many, many, many, new and exciting adventures.

ONIA AND TONIA

On a planet in a far off galaxy lives two little girls named Onia and Tonia. They live with their big brother, Bedron, who worked as a space car salesman.

One day their brother lost his job and though he tried he could not find another one. Day after day went by and he still found no job. Soon he began to be mean to Onia and Tonia. He would yell at them for nothing and spank them if they did anything bad.

Each day Onia and Tonia's brother would fly off in his space car to look for another job and each day he got meaner and meaner. As time went on he ran out of money and before long there was no more food in the house to eat. They also had no lights and no heat because he could no longer pay the utility bills. Onia and Tonia's brother blamed them for all their problems.

One day he told them, “I’m going to have to sell you two at the space slave market. Tomorrow, I'm going to take you to the planet Venderion and sell you so that I will have money to eat, to get the lights turned back on and the heat as well.”

Onia and Tonia were scared, but Onia, who was a year older, was busy trying to figure out how to keep from getting sold as a space slave. When they were in bed Onia pretended to be asleep but she did not sleep that night. She stayed up all night thinking of a way to get back home from wherever they would be taken.

Just before daylight Onia remembered something. She climbed out of her bed and walked softly to her brother's room where he was in a deep sleep. Underneath his bed she found what she was looking for-a tiny electronic disc. Her brother had explained that it was a GPS programmed disc which would pick up a signal from their house and no matter where you were in space the disc would pick up the signal and lead you back to the house.

She took the tiny disc, hurried back to her room and climbed back into bed.

Soon the morning sun shone and Onia and Tonia's brother came in to wake them up.

"It's a good day to become space slaves," he said to Onia and Tonia. "You should be happy, at least the people I sell you to will feed you, keep you warm and you won't be in the dark when the two suns go down. If you stay here you'll have nothing at all and neither will I."

But Onia and Tonia were not happy. Bedron made them put on their space travel suits and they followed him outside to his space car. Once the three of them were in, Bedron flew the space car up into the purple sky, through the clouds, into the darkness of outer space.

Onia guessed that the planet Venderion was not too far away because space cars were not built to go a long way in outer space. If the planet was very far Bedron would have used his spaceship.

As the space car whooshed through space Onia tried to get Tonia to stop crying. “Don’t worry little sister, everything will be okay,” Onia said.

For an hour they flew, and then Bedron began to guide the space car to a strange-looking grey planet.

“Well we’re here,” Bedron said. “The Venderion Space Slave Market. I hope I get a good price for you two. Who knows maybe one day I'll be able to buy you back."

Bedron knew he might not ever be able to buy them back and it made him feel sad. Deep down, he still loved his little sisters. He didn't really want to sell them, and hoped they would end up in a good home where they taken care of well.

As he got closer to the planet he began to slow the space car down. Soon buildings could be seen and everything looked cold and grey. Bedron guided the space car to the tallest building, flew through a large door, and landed inside the building. Onia and Tonia were frightened. Strange looking creatures were everywhere - in cages, in chains, and tied to walls. A man or woman stood beside each group of strange creatures and Onia guessed they were selling the creatures as slaves.

Soon an obese diminutive man wearing a green policeman's uniform came up to the space car.

"Welcome to the Space Slave Market of Venderion. I am Oyo. I am in charge of today's selling. What do you have to sell? I see no creatures."

"I'm selling these two little girls," said Bedron.

"These two? That is great!" said Oyo. "We do not get many little girls to sell these days. Most people are selling and buying space creatures, not humans. Yes, these two will bring a high price. Yes, indeed."

"How much do you think I can get?" asked Bedron.

"Why, I would buy them myself for at least 20,000 creditrons and I am not a rich man." Oyo replied, rubbing his big fat hands together. "A rich person will pay much more. When it is selling time we will find out how much more. I will do you a favor and put them on sale first."

Oyo turned and left and went over to a microphone hanging from the ceiling. The men and women began to gather around.

"Good buyers, I am Oyo, your seller today. I welcome you to the Space Slave Market of Venderion. We will begin today's selling with a special treat," he said, "two little girls."

The people all cheered and clapped their hands.

Bedron grabbed Onia and Tonia by their wrists and pulled them over to where Oyo was standing.

"Ah, here they are," Oyo said. "Aren't they pretty? They look good and strong so they will be able to do much work for you. We will begin the bidding by asking for 20,000 creditrons each."

"20,000," one man said.

"25,000," said another.

"30,000," said yet another.

And on and on it went until a very beautiful woman stood and said, “500,000 creditrons apiece.”

After that the other buyers got quiet.

“Sold,” said Oyo joyfully. “Sold to the pretty lady in the red spacesuit for 500,000 creditrons apiece.”

The pretty lady in the red spacesuit came up to where Onia, Tonia and Bedron were standing with Oyo.

“Who do I pay?” she asked.

“Me,” said Bedron, quickly putting out his hand.

Inside her spacesuit was a black plastic card, which she took out and punched a few buttons on the card.

“Here you are,” she said to Bedron handing him the black plastic card. “Take this to your bank and have them run it through their computer. One million creditrons will be taken from my bank and put into your account."

Tonia started to cry again and Onia was afraid she would never be able to use the electronic disc to find their way back home, so she began to cry too.

But, the woman paid no attention to the weeping and Bedron took the black plastic card. He also had tears in his eyes.

"You two go with this woman," said Bedron to Onia and Tonia. "You belong to her now, and stop bawling. She looks like a nice lady and I'm sure she will give you a better home than I could."

The woman in the red spacesuit grabbed Onia and Tonia by their arms and pulled them away. They screamed and kicked and tried to pull their arms free but the woman was too strong.

Again and again, they begged Bedron not to sell them but he walked away, tears now streaming down his cheeks. He climbed back into his space car. As Bedron guided the space car up and out the large door he looked into his reflection screen. His eyes were red and puffy. He cried and cried and cried. He really felt bad about selling Onia and Tonia but he couldn't see any other way to get the money he needed and find them a good home.

Now he was a rich man, but without his sisters he felt very poor.

The woman in the red spacesuit pulled Onia and Tonia behind her and went down a long dark hallway. The two girls had stopped trying to get away now. Besides, where would they go if they did? Bedron was gone, and even though they still had the electronic GPS disc they didn’t have a spaceship, a space car or even a skycle to fly back home. Both of them continued to cry.

Onia had hoped that this pretty lady would be kind to them or they would be able to get away someway, someday, somehow.

"My name is Maridron," the woman said. "I am your new master. You are my new slaves. Do what I tell you to do, when I tell you to do it, and we will get along just fine."

Onia and Tonia did not like her. As soon as turned to walk away from the Space Slave Market she started to change from a beautiful woman to a very old and scraggly hag. She looked like a Wormhole Witch! Her voice went from sounding like music to sounding like the croaking of a frog.

When the three of them got to the end of a long dark hallway they went through another door and stepped into a spaceship. Onia began to worry because Maridron had come to the Space Slave Market in a spaceship; so her planet must be a long way from their home.

Once inside the spaceship Maridron told Onia and Tonia to sit down in two chairs against the wall and buckle their seat belts. Then Maridron sat down in front of a large screen and what looked like a table with flashing buttons and lights on it.

Soon the spaceship began to move and go faster and faster until they were flying through space. They flew and flew and flew. The ride was much longer than the one they took to get to the Space Slave Market.

Tonia had cried herself to sleep and Onia acted like she was also asleep. But, her eyes were open a bit, watching Maridron to see how she operated the spaceship. Then, the spaceship began to slow down and Onia fully opened her eyes to see a planet on the screen. The planet got closer and closer and the spaceship went down to it. Onia touched Tonia so that her sister would awaken.

Onia could now see buildings. All of them were pink. Everything was pink! The sun, the sky, the trees, the grass; everything.

"Welcome to Pink Planet. This city is called the Candy Capitol," said Maridron. "Our people specialize in making good things to eat. Everything you see is made of a special kind of candy. And, as you can tell we make all of our candy pink."

Like all little girls, Onia and Tonia loved candy and both of them liked the idea of being on a planet where everything was made of candy. Maybe being a space slave on a candy planet wasn't such a bad thing.

Onia guessed Maridron had bought her and Tonia to put them to work making candy. Her mouth watered at the thought.

Maridron guided the spaceship around the back of the building and it whirred until it landed on the ground next to a lot of other spaceships.

Maridron got up from her place and told Onia and Tonia to follow her. They did and the three of them went inside the tall building.

They all walked over to the pink elevators and rode up and up and up until they reached the top. Maridron led them down a short pink hallway to a pink door and they went inside. All the furniture was pink, the rug was pink, the walls were pink; everything was pink. Onia and Tonia both smiled and said how pretty everything looked.

Maridron pointed both of them to a small room and told them to sit down. When they did she came to the door with a pink box in her hand and pushed a flashing pink button. Then a pink beam of light came on in the doorway to the room.

“This is a force field. Do not try to leave this room because you can’t get through the force field. Sit down and relax. I’ll bring you two some food.” Maridron said, and then she left.

Soon Maridron came back with a tray full of food surrounded by all the candy two little girls could eat. She pushed the button on the pink box again and the pink beam of light in the doorway was gone. She placed the tray on a small table in the room and went back outside. Once again, she pushed the button and the pink beam of light came on.

Onia and Tonia had forgotten how hungry they were until they saw the food and the two of them began to eat everything on the tray.

“Yes, my little sweet treats; eat, eat, eat all you want.

There is plenty where that comes from. I want you both to be good and fat when the time comes. Yes, I see you two are going to be worth every creditron I spent on you."

Onia wondered why Maridron had spent so much to buy them.

"Why did you spend so much to buy us?" she asked, between the bites of pink candy.

"Let's just say that I got tired of the same old candy," laughed Maridron. "I want something different."

Onia did not know what Maridron was talking about, but didn't like the way she was laughing.

"What do you mean?" she asked.

"Everyone in Candy Capitol is a candy maker and we have a contest every century to try and see who can make the best candy. Many different things are put in. But, I plan to make a brand new candy and win our next big

Centennial Candy Contest! I think there is one thing that will make the best candy in the world; something made of sugar, spice and everything nice-little girls!" Maridron cackled.

She was going to use them as candy ingredients!

Onia and Tonia stopped eating and grabbed each other, their little eyes wide with fear.

"No, no," they begged, "please don't turn us into candy. Please, we'll do anything, please!"

But, Maridron didn't listen. Her mind was made up.

"I paid one million creditrons so that I could put you two into my new batch of candy and win that contest and that is exactly what I am going to do. As soon as your weight is right, into the candy mixer you go."

Onia and Tonia cried and cried and cried but Maridron only laughed in her frog voice and left.

The next day she came and removed Onia from the

little room and told her to stand on the scale. Little red lights flashed and a number appeared.

"You need to gain ten more pounds," said Maridron. "I will save your little sister for another batch and you will be turned into candy first. But, first you must weigh enough and each day you will get fatter and fatter eating all food and candy a little girl can eat."

So each day Maridron would come to the little room with large trays of food and candy and though Onia and Tonia tried to stop themselves they ate all the food and candy.

At night, Maridron would come and put Onia on the scale to see if she was the right weight for her next batch of candy.

Onia was gaining a pound everyday and soon she was only one pound away from being just right for

Maridron's new batch of candy. It was then that she remembered something else about the electronic disc. If you turned it on any digital numbers in the room would read backwards!

That night Maridron came to the little room and placed Onia on the scale and just before he did she turned on the electronic disc.

"What is this," roared Maridron. "Yesterday, you weighed 54 pounds, today you weigh 45! This will never do! You must weigh 55 pounds exactly before I can use you in my next batch of candy. Maybe you need to eat a little more each day."

The next day Maridron brought more trays of food and candy but knowing she would be turned into candy if she gained another pound, Onia did not eat. Tonia ate all the food but she was so little it would be a very long time before she weighed enough to be put into

Maridron's new batch of candy. So when Maridron came down to weigh Onia she still weighed 54 pounds and the scale said 45. And it went on like that for a while, but one day she put Onia on the scale and Onia had lost a pound so that now her real weight was 53 pounds but the scale read 35 pounds. Maridron then understood that the scale must be wrong and that the numbers were reading backwards.

"I need a new scale," Maridron croaked, "This one seems to be reading backwards. But you are still two pounds too light for the batch of candy I want to make. I won't let that stop me from making my candy. If you won't get big enough then I'll just make a smaller batch of candy."

Tonia began to cry loudly and beg Maridron not to turn her big sister into candy. She didn't know what she would do without Bedron and Onia.

"I'm tired of your crying," Maridron said to her. "I'm going to put you too into my new batch of candy and be done with both of you. My batch will be bigger than I could make with just one of you."

Now Onia and Tonia began to cry and scream, but Maridron only turned and left, laughing uncontrollably.

Soon she came back with a pink apron on.

"My candy batch mixer is ready for you," she said, as she pushed the button on the pink box. "Come with me."

Maridron pulled the two little girls down a hallway into the kitchen. Next to the pink oven stood a pink machine with a round pink glass door. Inside was something pink being stretched and pulled like bubblegum.

"This is my candy mixer," said Maridron, "Once you two are inside I'll have the best batch of candy on the planet. I'm sure to win the contest!"

Then she grabbed Onia and began to drag her to the candy mixer. As she opened the door the candy mixer stopped. When she reached for Onia to put her in Onia fell to the floor moaning loudly, acting like she was fainting. She winked at Tonia.

Tonia remembered the trick they used to play on their brother Bedron, Onia would act like she was fainting and Tonia would push Bedron over Onia and make him fall. So, with all her tiny might she ran and pushed Maridron as she was trying to get Onia off the floor. The push made Maridron trip over Onia and fall into the candy mixer!

With Maridron in the mixer the candy turned from pink to sour green and the room soon smelled like rotten eggs.

Onia and Tonia ran from the place to the elevator

and Maridron's space ship. Onia sat at the table with the flashing lights. She knew which buttons to push because she had watched Maridron when she was pretending to be asleep.

The spaceship lifted up off the ground and before long they had left Pink Planet and were speeding through space. Onia turned on the GPS electronic disc and guided the ship by the disc's beeping.

Soon they saw their home planet on the screen and Onia guided the ship to their house and landed.

Bedron's eyes were filled with joy when he saw them. He had blubbered and whimpered and wailed everyday since the day he had sold them. He told them that even though he was now a rich man he had not been happy. Money could never replace the love he had for his two pretty little sisters.

They forgave their brother for his mistake and told

him about Maridron and the Pink Planet and how they got away.

The three of them were very happy to be together as a family again and they hugged and kissed each other. Now they were all rich.

They had everything they needed and decided to use their new wealth to help others in need.

Thanks to Maridron's money, they would never have to worry about money again. Onia and Tonia both smiled as they slept that night and they and their brother were ensured of a generous future together.

TRONINA

On a planet in a far off galaxy there lives a little girl named Tronina.

One day Tronina wanted to play. Everyone in the house was doing something else and no one wanted to play with her.

Tronina went into her parents' bedroom where her mother was making the bed. She picked up a pillowcase.

"Tronina! Don't touch that pillowcase," said her mother. "You will get it wrinkled and I will have to change the bed again."

Tronina's mother went back to making the bed. "Why don't you go outside and play, Tronina?" she said.

Tronina went downstairs and outside. Her big sister Mar-Lyn was playing with her robot-doll.

Tronina went over to the robot-doll and touched it.

"Leave my robot-doll alone," said her sister. "That is my robot-doll and you have your own. Now get away, before you mess up the lights or something."

Tronina felt like crying.

"My robot-doll is very old and very special," said Mar-Lyn softly, seeing that Tronina's feelings were hurt. "If you mess it up, I may not be able to get it fixed. Don't ever touch it again, okay?"

Tronina just looked at Mar-Lyn.

Why don't you go inside and see what our brother is doing, Tronina," Mar-Lyn said.

Tronina went inside and upstairs to her big brother's room. There in the middle of the floor her big brother, Se-Tan, was fixing his skycle for the weekly skycle races.

Tronina went over and picked up one of his tools.

"Tronina!" he shouted. "What are you doing? Get away from my tools. You will have them all over the place and I won't be able to find them."

Again, Tronina wanted to cry.

"Now go play somewhere else, Tronina!" Se-Tan yelled. "I have work to do here and you are slowing me down. I have to work fast to get my skycle ready."

Tronina just looked at Se-Tan.

"Now get out of my room, ordered Se-Tan. "Go play with someone else."

Tronina went down to the basement where her father was working on the family computer.

Tronina stood beside the machine and watched for a while. Her father sat in front of the computer pushing icons as the machine whirred and clicked.

Then Tronina reached out to push an icon.

"Tronina!" said her father. "How many times have I told you not to touch the computer. You are not yet old enough to work it and you have not learned what to do."

"Teach me, please," said Tronina.

"I don't have time right now," said her father. "I have lots of work to do. Go and play with your brother or sister."

This time Tronina did wail. She stood there and whined out loud and cried and cried some more.

Her mother heard the crying and came running downstairs followed by Mar-Lyn and Se-Tan, who had also heard the loud noise.

"What's wrong with Tronina?" said her father.

"I'm not sure but I have an idea," said her mother.

"Me too," said Mar-Lyn.

"Me too," replied Se-Tan.

"We have all been so busy today we forgot to show her how much we love her and love having her with us. We forgot that the most valuable thing we can give her and each other is our time." Tronina's mother said, as she picked her up and kissed and hugged her. Tronina held her tightly, sobbing softly.

"Tronina. if you're not too busy, there is something you can help me with in the kitchen," said her mother.

Tronina stopped crying and smiled a big smile.

Her mother carried her to the kitchen and her father, sister and brother followed them.

Then Tronina's mother pulled out a big bowl of purple peanuts and gave it to Tronina.

"I am about to make some purple peanut butter cookies," said Tronina's mother. "You can help me take the shell off the peanuts."

"That's a good idea." said her father.

"She's not to little to do that," said her sister.

"That's right," said her brother.

"No," said her mother. "She's perfect in every way and she will always be perfect to all of us."

Tronina sat on the kitchen floor taking the shell off the purple peanuts. Now she was very happy because she knew in the future to remember that no matter how busy they were, everyone in her family thought she was perfect and loved her very much.

STARZON - THE SPACE ORPHAN

On a planet in a far off galaxy lives a young man named Starzon. When Starzon was a young boy he lived with his mommy and daddy on another planet. His mother was very pretty. She taught school at the Space Scholar School. His father was a famous scientist. One day Starzon’s father came home looking very scared.

“What’s the matter father?” asked Starzon.

“I’m afraid our planet is doomed,” said Starzon's father. “War has been declared on us by the Galaxian Gargantuans.”

“Who are the Galaxian Gargantuans?” little Starzon wanted to know.

“They are giants, bad and ugly creatures who live on the other side of the Summer Star. They spend their whole lives declaring war on other planets and destroying them. I never thought we would have to fight them, but we do. They’re on their way here to blow up our planet right now!”

“Yes, father we will fight them!” said Starzon, holding up his two tiny fists in a fighting pose.

“No, no, my brave little soldier,” Starzon's father laughed. “You are too young to fight them. You must hide.”

“But father, said Starzon. “Where will I hide? If the Galaxian Gargantuans blow up our planet there will be no place to hide.

“Yes there is one place. Follow me.”

Starzon's father led him down the winding metal steps to his laboratory.

He pointed at an odd-looking purple box in the corner.

"You will hide in there," he said.

"But Father, what is this purple box?" Starzon asked.

"This box is something I have been working on for a long time. It is made of metal so strong that nothing can bend it or break it. It will protect you if we get blown up by the Galaxian Gargantuans."

"Will you and Mommy hide with me?" asked Starzon.

"No my son, we cannot," replied his father. "The purple box is too small. I was able to make enough of the special metal to build a box big enough only for you. Your mother and I will have to stay upstairs and fight. So get into the box and don't come out no matter what you hear. We love you."

"But Father, I want to stay with you and Mommy," Starzon pleaded.

"I'm sorry my son but you must understand I am putting you in this box to keep you alive. If the Galaxian Gargantuans destroy our planet this purple box will float in space until someone finds you."

"But I don't want to live without you and Mommy," Starzon cried.

"You must live my son. You are the future," his father said, as he too cried. "You can help make the universe a better place and maybe one day get rid of the Galaxian Gargantuans forever!"

Starzon's father opened the lid of the purple box and pulled a glowing triangle on a golden chain out of his pocket.

"Oh, I almost forgot," said the scared scientist.

"Here is the Neon Native Necklace I made especially for you."

When he put the Neon Native Necklace around Starzon's neck it began to glow on, then off, then on again.

"This necklace will glow on and off only when it is on your neck. It is just like the ones the grown-ups on our planet wear. You were not supposed to have yours until you grew up but I think you should have yours now. The necklace will grow up with you."

"Goodbye my son," he said. He kissed Starzon and hugged him tightly. "I want you to grow up and be good and strong. Find yourself a beautiful wife and have ten beautiful children, as beautiful as you are! I only wish your mother would get here. She hasn't come back from the Space Scholarship School yet. I hope she makes it back in time to say goodbye to you.

But if she doesn't, always remember nobody loves you like your mother and I do. Remember us."

Starzon still resisted getting into the purple box so his father lifted him up, put him in and closed the top, telling him that once locked it could only be opened from the inside.

Starzon's father hugged him again and continued to cry as he locked the box and went back upstairs.

The box was small inside. It was just big enough for Starzon to sit down. A light filled the box but Starzon didn't know where it was coming from. It was just all around and not coming from one place.

By the light Starzon could see his tears begin dropping on the floor of the purple box.

As he sat there sobbing he heard loud noises that sounded like bombs! The sounds kept getting louder and louder, so loud Starzon could not hear himself crying anymore.

He was so scared! He curled himself up into a little ball and covered his ears.

Then he heard one loud boom! The box flew up in the air and begun spinning around and around. Starzon heard screams and more loud noises. Boom! Boom! Boom! The purple box was tossed this way and that way.

Then the noise stopped.

The purple box started spinning very slowly and Starzon could tell he was now floating in space. He knew he would never see his parents again.

He floated there in outer space, the box spinning around and around and around. It was so quiet now. The only thing Starzon could hear was his own crying. He cried and cried and cried until he cried himself to sleep.

A space traveler spotted the floating purple box while on his way home to his planet.

“What is this funny looking purple box?” he said. “I’ve never seen anything like it. I’d like to see what’s in it.”

The space traveler’s name was Leezak. Leezak pushed a button and a long metal robot arm came from the side of his spaceship. He slowed down until he came close enough and the robot arm grabbed the purple box. The robot arm pulled the box into Leezak’s spaceship.

Once it was inside, Leezak looked the purple box over. Then he began to tap it on the top. Tap! Tap! Tap! The noise woke Starzon. He thought the noise was from flying space rocks hitting against the floating box. But, then he realized the box wasn't floating anymore.

Leezak heard Starzon moving inside the box.

“What is in there?” he said. He was afraid there

might be a strange space monster inside, so he pulled out his laser gun and pointed it at the purple box.

"I said what's in there!" Leezak demanded.

Starzon heard the man's voice but he was afraid to open the box. The voice sounded mean and angry. He started crying.

Leezak then knew there was a person inside. He tried to find a way to open the box but he could not. There was no way. He guessed the box could only be opened from the inside.

"All right, whoever you are in there. You better come out right now or I'll blast this purple box to little pieces. I'm counting to three," said Leezak, if you want to live you better come out then or this laser gun will be the end of you."

Leezak counted to three, "One! Two! Three!" As soon as he did he began firing the laser gun at the purple box. He fired. He fired again. But he could not put a dent in the purple box Starzon's father built.

Starzon knew the box was too strong for any laser gun but the loud noise inside the box when the shots hit it scared him. Again, he began to cry.

"I don't know what or who is in there but if you don't come out I will put you and this purple box back into space!"

Starzon did not want to continue floating around in space. He would face the angry man instead.

Starzon opened the box.

Leezak was very surprised to see the little boy with the tears on his face.

"Who are you little boy?" he said. "What are you doing in this box floating around in outer space?"

Starzon told the man about his father and mother and how his father locked him in the box to protect him from the Galaxian Gargantuans who had destroyed his home planet.

"Oh, that is so sad," said Leezak. "You are too young to lose your parents."

Leezak didn't seem nearly as mean as his voice sounded from inside the purple box. Starzon soon started to like him and the he wasn't afraid any more.

"Your father must have loved you very much to build such a strong box to protect you," Leezak said. "Anything so strong must be built with love."

Starzon began to cry again.

"Yes, my father loved me and my mother did too. I loved them too! I miss them so much. I wish I were dead too."

"You must never wish that!" snapped Leezak. "Be careful what you wish for. One of the Mysterious Maidens from Mars might hear you and grant your wish. No, don't ever wish to die! Wish to live! Think about your father! You think he went to the trouble of making that purple box for you if he didn't want you to live? Don't let your family down! You must stay alive for your lost family. Your father and mother did not wish to die and I know they would not want you to wish you were dead."

"But what do I have to live for?" exclaimed Starzon. "I have no mother, no father, no home, not even a planet to live on."

"I'll take you to my home planet and you can make that your home. You can grow up there. I'm sure we can find someone who wants a handsome little boy like you. Maybe my Master will even let you stay at our house. He has a little boy too. There is always something to live for, if you look."

"Your master"? asked Starzon. "Who is that?"

"I am a servant who lives and works in the house of the famous Lord La-Dron on the planet Timor. I was on an errand for him when I saw your purple box floating out there in space."

"Is your master nice?" Starzon wanted to know.

"He is a very busy man and sometimes he does not seem to be so nice but that is because he is so busy. But, you must be careful of his son. He is not so nice."

When they got to Leezak's planet, Starzon was amazed at how big the city was and he was even more amazed to see a giant plexi-glass space station floating above the city.

"Does your master live on that space station?" he asked.

"No young one," replied Leezak, "that is the space station of the Centurion, the most powerful man on our planet, Timor. He lives there with his beautiful daughter, Celestica. She is just about your age."

"Have you ever been there?" asked Starzon.

"No, never," replied Leezak. "The only servants allowed there are the ones that work for the Centurion. No others are allowed."

"Do you think I could go there someday?"

"I don't know Starzon," said Leezak. "If my master lets you stay with us he may make you a servant or adopt you as a son of his own. If he makes you a servant you can never go there."

By then Leezak was landing his spaceship on a high building.

"We're here," said Leezak. "Remember what I told you about my master's son. He is not a nice boy and if the boy doesn't like you, my master may not like you either. So, stay away from my master's bad little son."

As the doors of the spaceship whooshed open

Starzon and Leezak came face to face with Leezak's master and his son.

"Leezak! Where have you been?" demanded Lord La-Dron. How long does it take you to run one simple errand? And who is this boy with you?"

"This is Starzon," Leezak said. And he told his master how he found the boy in a purple box floating around in open space after the Galaxian Gargantuans had destroyed his planet.

"That is too bad," said Lord La-Dron. "He looks to be the same age as my son. I've always wanted another son. Maybe I'll adopt him as my son and make him the son of a Lord."

"Yes sir!" smiled Leezak. "That is what I was hoping. He is such a smart and handsome boy. He will make you a fine son."

"Yes, I think so," Leezak's master said. "I, Lord

La-Dron, will now have two sons, Au-Gron and Starzon!"

Lord La-Dron looked down at his own son standing next to him.

"He's not so great," mumbled Au-Gron. "I want to see his purple box."

"Yes! I would like to see his purple box too. Leezak, get the box from the ship so we may see it."

Leezak went back into the ship and returned with the purple box.

Lord La-Dron and his cruel son Au-Gron had never seen anything like it and they did not know what it was made of.

"You say this box won't even bend under laser gun blasts?" said Lord La-Dron to Leezak.

"Yes Master, it even protected Starzon from the bombs of the Galaxian Gargantuans."

"We must study this and see what it is made of." said Lord La-Dron. "For now Starzon, welcome to my family."

Two weeks or so passed and Starzon was beginning to like being the son of Lord La-Dron. He had lots of good food, nice clothes, and his own room with a big soft bed, and all the toys he could play with. But he didn't like Au-Gron. Au-Gron played tricks on Starzon whenever he got the chance. Starzon had not seen Leezak much lately but did not mind it since he began to think the son of a Lord should not have servants as friends.

One day the two boys were in the garden in back of the house and Au-Gron was trying to think of a new bad trick to play on Starzon.

He was about to squirt ink on Starzon's nice new shirt when Lord La-Dron came out of the house.

"Starzon," he said. "I have checked out your purple box and my scientists know most of what it is made. But there is something extra in there and they don't know what it is. Do you know?"

"Leezak said that it was made with love," Starzon replied.

Lord La-Dron laughed. "Love? How do you make a box and put love in it?"

"I don't know," said Starzon, "but I know my Mommy and Daddy loved me enough to find a way."

"Well, anyway," said Lord La-Dron, "you can have the box back now. We don't have any use for it and you might as well keep it as a toy or to remind you of your family."

"I want it." said Au-Gron. "Give me the box, Daddy."

"No! You can't have it," said Starzon running to

grab the box.

"I want it," said Au-Gron angrily. "Make him give it to me Daddy."

"Well, how about it Starzon," said Lord La-Dron. "Can Au-Gron have your little purple box?"

"No! He can't have it. It's mine!" said Starzon. My father made it just for me!"

"Make him give it to me Daddy! I want it real bad, said Au-Gron, smiling, as he pretended to cry.

Lord La-Dron didn't know what to do. He had never denied Au-Gron anything that he wanted. He wasn't about to start now.

"Yes, Au-Gron you can have the box," said Lord La-Dron.

"No! Why are you trying to give him my box?" demanded Starzon. "It's mine. My father built it for me. It's not his."

"If I say it is his, it is his!" yelled Lord La-Dron. "He's my son and he wants it, so he shall have it. It's only a box. It saved your life and has no use to you now."

"It's not just any box! It reminds me of my family and my father built it just for me. He put love in it just for me, not for Au-Gron."

"Look Starzon," Lord La-Dron said sternly. "I said the box is now Au-Gron's. He is my son and he wants it. I said he can have it. That's the end of it!"

"But you said I was your son too!" said Starzon.

"Yes I know," replied Lord La-Dron, "but Au-Gron is my real son. He is a true La-Dron. He will carry my name on when I'm gone. You are not my real son. You do not carry my name. I only let you become my son because you lost your real parents. But Au-Gron comes first. If he wants something he must have it."

"I won't give it to him." said Starzon.

"It is not your choice!" Lord La-Dron's voice boomed. "I decide who gets what, when, where, how and how much in this house, not you, and I say the box now in the property of Au-Gron!"

"No! I won't let you take my purple box. I don't care who you are!" yelled Starzon.

"You don't care? YOU don't care?" laughed Lord La-Dron. "How dare you come into my house and disobey me! I am Lord La-Dron. You little space orphan! When you came here I could have made you a servant but I took you in and treated you like a son. Now you dare tell me you don't care what I say!"

"Guards! Guards!" he called. Two uniformed men appeared almost before he had finished the words.

"Take this little space orphan to Leezak in the servants' quarters downstairs. He is no longer my son.

He has not been a good son. He is now a servant and if he is not a good servant I'll do away with him!"

The guards took Starzon away and he heard Au-Gron snickering as the guards pulled him.

When the guards brought him to Leezak they opened the door and threw Starzon on the floor.

"What happened?" asked Leezak. Starzon told Leezak what had happened.

When he was finished Leezak was crying.

"Why are you crying?" asked Starzon.

"I had hoped that you would be able to see the inside of the Centurion's Space Station one day. I've always wanted to see what it was like but I knew I would never get to see it. I thought that if you got to see it you could tell me about it. That way, I could see it through your eyes. But now, I guess I won't even get that," said Leezak.

Starzon felt sorry for Leezak. But he also felt sorry for himself for now he was a servant.

From then on Au-Gron made sure Starzon worked hard everyday. He played tricks on Starzon too and got him into trouble whenever he could.

Sometimes Au-Gron made Starzon so mad that he would sit in his little servant's room and cry. Sometimes he would feel like he had nothing to live for. But, whenever he felt that way he would think of his father and mother and how much they loved him. He knew they wanted him to live.

As the years passed, Starzon grew into a big strong young man. He still worked and worked and worked.

Au-Gron never worked. He spent most of his time telling Starzon what to do. His favorite past time was messing up his own room and making Starzon clean it up.

One day Au-Gron was laying on his bed watching Starzon clean up the room for the third time that day. Au-Gron was making fun of Starzon's clothes which were now those of a servant.

Au-Gron grabbed his remote control device and turned on the big screen monitor on his wall. A man with a solid gold uniform was on the screen.

"To all Lords and Ladies of the planet Timor the Annual Centurion's Cotillion will be held on the usual star date. All Lords and Ladies are expected to be there on time. This is the year the Centurion's daughter, Celestica, will pick a husband. All eligible Lords should be at their best!"

Au-Gron clicked off the monitor with the remote control.

"How would you like to go to the Centurion's Cotillion," he said to Starzon.

"Don't kid me, Au-Gron," said Starzon. "You know I've always wanted to go. You say the same thing to me every year. You know you or Lord La-Dron would never let me go."

"Lord La-Dron does what I tell him to do," laughed Au-Gron. "as you well know from the time I had him give me your little purple box. If I say I want you to go my Father will allow it. He gives me anything I want."

Starzon almost started crying when he thought about the purple box. But he did not, knowing that would only have made Au-Gron happy.

"I'll tell you what Starzon," said Au-Gron. "I'll make sure you can go to the Centurion's Cotillion if you have royal clothes to wear. You have to be dressed to impress!"

"You know I have no such clothes," said Starzon.

"Why do you tease me and try to hurt me like this every year?"

"You don't believe me? Wait a minute!" Au-Gron grabbed the remote control and clicked the button. Lord La-Dron appeared on the screen. "What is it my son?" he asked.

"I want Starzon to go to the Centurion's Cotillion this year. He is a young man now. It's about time he saw the Centurion's Space Station."

"What is this Au-Gron? said Lord La-Dron. "Haven't you gotten tired of that joke you play on Starzon every year?"

"I'm serious this time, Father."

"Look Au-Gron," Lord La-Dron said angrily, "you know servants are not allowed on the Centurion's Space Station, unless they work for him."

"We'll dress him up in royal clothes. Who'll know

the difference?" said Au-Gron.

"I'm tired of this game, Au-Gron!" Lord La-Dron yelled. "This time I am going to let him go. I'm not going to let you change your mind this year. Starzon can go! You give him a suit of royal clothes from your closet."

With that Lord La-Dron disappeared from the screen.

Au-Gron knew he had gone too far. Lord La-Dron was serious about letting Starzon go to the Centurion's Cotillion.

"Well, well," he chuckled, "so you are going this year. My father told me to get you a suit from my closet. But he didn't say it had to be a good one!"

He got off the bed and went to the revolving closet. He opened the door.

Rows of royal suits in all colors hung there

spinning slowly. Starzon had seen them before and he smiled at the thought of wearing one, and finally getting to see the Centurion's Space Station. He couldn't wait to tell Leezak!

Au-Gron walked into the closet looking from side to side. Soon he stopped and bent over to pick up something off the floor.

"Here is your suit, Starzon, A royal rag for a royal servant. Celestica will surely pick you!" he laughed.

The old suit was little ragged and very dirty. It looked like it had been lying in the corner of the closet for a long, long time. But Starzon thought it was good enough. It just needed to be cleaned and patched a bit. Just then Au-Gron began pulling at the suit, tearing the arms off and ripping the pockets. When he was done he threw the torn clothes to Starzon and walked out of the room.

For a moment he turned around. “One more thing, if you’re thinking about getting it fixed, don’t bother! I’m going to keep you so busy you won’t have time,” he said.

Starzon took the old torn and dirty suit to his servant’s room. Seven Space Spiders lived in Starzon's room.

They were his best friends next to Leezak. He had looked for Leezak to tell him the news but could not find him.

“I’m going to Centurion’s Cotillion this year, for real!” he told the Seven Space Spiders.

“That’s wonderful,” they said. Then he showed them the torn and dirty suit of royal clothes.

“If I can just get this fixed and cleaned,” Starzon said. “If I only had some fine gold medals to pin on my chest.”

Starzon heard Au-Gron calling for him and he went back upstairs to see what he wanted.

"I want you to clean up my room again, and then clean the Cosmic Camel stable again, then take the garbage to the waste recycling plant again, and come back quickly to see what else I have thought of for you to do next!"

All that day and the next and the next, Au-Gron kept Starzon busy. He never had a moment's peace. When he did get a break all he could do was sleep.

The Seven Space Spiders wanted Starzon to get a chance to go to the Cotillion. So they all got together and decided to help Starzon get his suit ready for the Cotillion.

They took the suit and washed it good until it was sparkling clean. Then they spun silk threads and mended the tears and sewed the buttons back on. When they were done, it looked like a brand new suit!

Soon it was time to go to the Cotillion. Starzon was in Au-Gron's room helping him get dressed. “Did you get the royal suit ready in time?” Au-Gron asked.

“No I didn’t,” said Starzon sadly.

“Too bad. But, it’s just as well,” said Au-Gron with a big smile. “YOU have to learn to work faster.”

When Au-Gron was dressed he and Lord La-Dron went outside to get into Lord La-Dron’s shiny new space car, leaving Starzon behind.

Starzon went to his dim servant’s room. When he opened the door he saw the beautiful suit of royal clothes the Seven Space Spiders had fixed for him! It was the best suit of royal clothes he had ever seen. He put it on. Then he ran over to the window.

“I have a suit. I can go with you!” he yelled down to Au-Gron and Lord La-Dron, who were just climbing into their space car.

Starzon ran outside. “Wait for me!” he said.

Au-Gron was amazed and also very mad. He got out of the space car. When Starzon tried to climb in, Au-Gron tripped him and Starzon fell into a large mud puddle!

“Oh well, too bad, so sad, for Starzon,” said Au-Gron, “I guess you still can’t go.” Au-Gron climbed into the space car and he and Lord La-Dron flew off.

Starzon could not help it. He began to cry.

“I wish I could go to the Cotillion,” said Starzon. “I wish, I wish, I wish, I wish.”

A Mysterious Maiden from Mars heard him wishing. She came down from the blue sky and spoke to him.

Starzon looked up. There stood a beautiful red-haired woman with a red glow all around her.

"I am a Mysterious Maiden from Mars," she said. "I will grant you your wish."

She blew a kiss at Starzon and the torn and dirty royal suit was like new again, but even better now. She blew him another kiss and a brand new space car appeared.

"You will go in style," she said. "I will make a robot driver for your new space car, four robot body guards, and two more robots to carry your royal cape. But I need some space spiders."

The Seven Space Spiders from Starzon's room were scared and they tried to hide.

But the Mysterious Maiden saw them and blew a kiss at them. One spider turned into a robot driver. The other six turned into four robot body guards plus two royal cape carriers. They all got into the space car.

Starzon climbed in between two of the robot body guards and off they went to the Centurion's Space

Station.

"There's one thing I forgot to tell you Starzon," the Mysterious Maiden yelled.

"The wish ends tonight at the time of the Eternal Eclipse."

Starzon heard her. He knew he would not be able to stay at the Cotillion all night but was glad to have even a little bit of time to enjoy his wish.

At the Cotillion the Centurion was angry.

"Celestica had met all the young Lords on the planet," the Centurion said, "and still she sees no one she likes."

Just then Starzon came into the room. He had put a mask on because he didn't want Au-Gron and Lord La-Dron to know who he was. When Celestica saw him she knew she wanted to meet this young man with the mask on. She and Starzon walked toward each other and without saying a word they began to dance. Starzon and Celestica danced and danced and danced. It was as if no one else was in the room. Au-Gron and all the other young Lords were jealous of the mysterious stranger. They asked each other who he was but no one knew. Starzon looked so different in his beautiful royal suit and purple mask. The time went by fast. Soon the whole room began to get dark and the digital clock on the wall began to buzz, the Eternal Eclipse had started.

Just then Starzon remembered he had to leave and started running to the door!

"Where are you going?" Celestica asked, running after him. But Starzon did not answer. He kept running to get to his space car.

Celestica reached for him as they ran but all she was able to grab was his Neon Native Necklace, the necklace his father had given to him when he put him in the purple box so many years before.

The necklace came off into her hand but Starzon ran on, jumped into his space car and was driven off by his robot driver. She looked at it and noticed it was not going on and off like it was when it was on Starzon's neck. So she knew that if she put the necklace on the right neck it would go on and off and she would find the mysterious stranger. She held it up into the light and showed it to the Centurion who had followed her to the launch bay.

"The man who wore this necklace is the man that will be my husband," she said. That night she took her robot guards and they went to the city below looking for Starzon. They went to every house.

Then they came to Lord La-Dron's house. Starzon was in his room. The wish had worn off and the Seven

Space Spiders were there with him.

Celestica asked Au-Gron to try the necklace on. He did but the necklace did not flash on and off. Disappointed again, Celestica was about to leave when Starzon came upstairs from his servant's room.

"Who is this?" asked Celestica.

"He's just a servant," said Au-Gron. Celestica was desperate.

"He must try it on also," she said.

Starzon tried on the necklace. It began to glow on and off, on and off, on and off.

"You are the man I want as my husband," Celestica said.

She and Starzon returned to the Centurion Space Station and were married in a glorious and beautiful ceremony.

Since he was now the Centurion's son-in-law,

Starzon was the second most powerful man on the planet Timor. So he went back to Lord La-Dron's house and took back his purple box. He also took Leezak back to the space station to reward him for being a great friend.

One day he became the Centurion and he, Celestica, Leezak and the Seven Space Spiders (and the little purple box made with love), now enjoy a wonderful life together.

BROWN BEAUTRON AND THE TITAN TRIPLETS

On a planet in a far off galaxy, lives a young woman named Beautron. When she was a little girl everyone called her Brown Beautron, because she had the brownest and prettiest face they had ever seen.

At that time Beautron lived with her older sister in one of the tallest buildings on the planet. The sister was also very brown and very pretty, but not as brown or pretty as Beautron.

The two of them got along very well. They talked and laughed and went almost everywhere together.

But, as Beautron began to get older she became browner and even prettier. Up to then, everybody had thought Beautron was a pretty girl, but now people began to see her as a beautiful woman.

Beautron's big sister, Beautina, became jealous of her because now Beautron was no longer just her cute little sister, but almost more beautiful. She began to think of Beautron as a rival.

One day Beautina had several flat boxes delivered. She placed them all in the living room and un-stacked them. They were full of wires, circuits and other machine parts. She had her servants put the pieces together.

When they were finished, she had a magnificent computer! It had many buttons and a huge touchscreen monitor.

When Beautron saw it, she was very happy. She

had always wanted a personal computer to play with. "Beautina," said Beautron, "I like this computer! What can it do?"

"It is a B-Q computer, Beautina said.

"What does B-Q stand for?" Beautron asked.

"B-Q stands for Beauty Quotient. The machine measures how much beauty there is on the entire planet and it can also say who the most beautiful woman on the planet is.

"Oh how exciting!" exclaimed Beautron. "Let's see if it works.

"Okay, let's!" said Beautina and she began pressing screen icons. The machine whirred and clicked. Then an electronic voice spoke. "Working," it said.

"Computer who is the most beautiful woman on the planet," said Beautina.

The computer whirred and clicked like a high speed

skycle. Then it stopped. “You, Beautina are the most beautiful woman on the planet,” said the computer.

Beautina smiled a wide smile.

“Can the computer also say who the second most beautiful woman on the planet is?” Beautron asked. “I'll bet it’s me!”

“Well let’s ask it,” said Beautina. “Computer who is the second most beautiful woman on the planet?” Again, the computer whirred and clicked very fast and stopped. “The second most beautiful woman on the planet is Maven Marizon.”

“Who is that?” said Beautron.

“I don't know,” Beautina answered.

Beautron was getting sad. She was sure the second most beautiful woman on the planet was her.

“I don't understand,” she cried. “Everybody always says that I am the brownest and prettiest girl they have ever seen. I must at least be number three." Again, Beautina asked the computer. Again, the answer was no.

Beautron knew something had to be wrong. "Surely, I am one of the prettiest women on the planet," she said. "If I am not number one, two or three, where do I fit in?"

"Computer is Beautron one of the prettiest women on the planet?" Without whirring or clicking, the computer said, "no."

"That's impossible," said Beautron and even Beautina agreed.

"Computer, why do you say Beautron is not one of the prettiest women on the planet?" said Beautina.

"She is not yet eighteen years, and not yet a woman. But when she becomes a woman she will be number one on our world.

That was it! Beautron was the most beautiful *girl* on the planet but she wasn't the most beautiful *woman* because she was not a woman yet.

Beautina did not want to hear anymore. She was mad, because she knew it would not be much longer before she would lose her place as the most beautiful woman on the planet.

Everyday she asked the computer and it gave the same answer. Beautina was still the most beautiful woman on the planet.

But one day, Beautron turned eighteen years-old and that day the computer gave a different answer, "Beautron is now the brownest and most beautiful woman on the planet."

Beautina was so mad she ran out of the house. She did not speak to anyone else she saw passing by on the moving sidewalks. Her mind was on Beautron.

She had to get rid of her. Beautina promised herself that somehow she would become the most beautiful woman on the planet once again.

As the sidewalk moved her along she came across a sly-looking young man standing in front of the video arcade.

"Why do you look so mad, beautiful one?" he said to Beautina. "Do you have a problem? My name is Slim Slak. Maybe I can help you."

"Maybe you can," she said to Slim Slak. "I'll pay you to get my sister off the planet and make sure she never comes back. You can drop her off so far away she can never return. Better yet, kill her. I must be the most beautiful once again!"

So Slim Slak agreed to take Beautron away. Beautina gave him 100,000 creditrons and told him how to find Beautron.

Slim Slak went to where Beautron and Beautina lived. When Beautron opened the door he grabbed her and stuffed her into a large bag! He carried her over his shoulder and put her in his space car and flew away as fast as he could. Soon they came to a large spaceship. Slim Slak took Beautron out of his space car and carried her aboard as she kicked and screamed. Once inside, he opened the bag she was in.

It was the first real good look he had a chance to get. He was stunned at how brown and beautiful she was. The thought of killing her made him sad. He was not sure he could go through with it.

"Why am I here?" demanded Beautron.

"You're here because your sister wants you away from this planet, as far away as possible. She said to kill you."

"I don't believe you," cried Beautron.

"Well it's true," laughed Slim Slak. But, I think you are too good-looking to kill. You are the brownest most beautiful woman I've ever seen. I think I'll just abandon you on a floating piece of space rock then I won't have to know what happens to you."

"Oh, please don't do that!" cried Beautron.

"I have to do something with you," Slim Slak said. "I made a deal with your sister and I always keep my word. So just relax. Who knows? Someone may come along and pick you up from your floating space rock before you die."

Beutron did not know what to do. She was scared. She looked around for someplace to run but there was no way out.

Slim Slak sat down at the spaceship's controls and began pushing buttons.

The spaceship began to hum loudly. Then it began to

rumble and shake.

"Better sit down and strap yourself into that chair over there," Slim Slak said to Beautron. "When the ship takes off you may float all around if you don't strap yourself in."

Beautron felt like crying. She did not want to strap herself into the chair. She didn't want to be on the ship at all. How could her big sister, Beautina do this to her? Everything seemed like one awful, terrible dream.

"I said strap yourself in!" shouted Slim Slak, and he sounded very serious.

Beautron thought that she had better do what he said or he might hurt her. So she went over to the other chair and strapped herself in.

As soon as she did the spaceship began to lift up and off the ground. Higher, higher, higher and higher still it flew until Beautron's planet looked like a tiny dot on the monitor screen. Then they could see it no more.

Beautron stared at the monitor screen. All she could see now were stars and wide open space.

"Where are you taking me?" Beautron asked.

"I don't know. There are some empty planets in our galaxy and I think I will take you to one of them and leave you there. That way you will have someplace to live for the rest of your life," Slim Slak answered.

"But I don't want to live anywhere else but my home planet," Beautron cried.

"Too bad brown and beautiful one," he replied. "Your sister does not want you there."

Now, Beautron began to cry.

"How could my sister do this to me?" she said. "Beauty is a funny thing," explained Slim Slak. "Many people have it on the outside, but they do not have it on the inside. Inside they are ugly and they do wicked things to people because they care more about their looks than they do about others' feelings."

"That is so wrong," Beautron said.

"Sure it is," said Slim Slak. "But that is the way it is. Some people are beautiful outside and ugly inside. Some people are ugly outside and beautiful inside. Some people are beautiful outside and inside. And, others still are ugly outside and inside. Everybody is one or the other."

"Which are you?" Beautron asked.

"Hmmm. I never really thought about it until now. I guess I'm ugly outside and beautiful inside."

"How can you be beautiful inside and just drop me off on some empty planet?"

"I was supposed to kill you," said Slim Slak. "I made a deal with your sister, but I am going to let you live. It is better to be alive on an empty planet than to be dead on a full one. So I think I am beautiful inside because I cannot bring myself to kill you."

"Then why don't you just take me back to my planet?" Beautron asked.

"Because I made a deal to get you away from there and make sure you can't get back. I keep my promises. Besides, if I take you back there you will always be in danger. Your sister will only find someone else to do what she asked me to do," he answered.

"I don't care," Beautron replied. "I'll die of loneliness on an empty planet."

"Loneliness takes a long time to kill you, while other ways of dying are very quick. Even though you will be lonely for people you will be alive. Besides, there are space creatures on most of the empty planets. They may make you less lonely," he replied, "and who knows some space explorer or a Twisted Time

Traveler may come along in a few years and rescue you.

But, if that happens you must never come back to your home planet or you will surely die a quick death!"

Slim Slak was starting to feel that he could not even drop the beautiful brown Beautron off on an empty planet where other people would not be able to enjoy her brownness and beauty.

A solar system of planets began to come into the monitor screen.

"Is that where you are taking me?" asked Beautron.

"No. All those planets have people on them and you could easily get back to your home planet from them. The planet I'm taking you to is much farther away."

Then Slim Slak had an idea. "I'm going to put the

ship on automatic pilot," he said. "I have to go to below and check my other cargo, and don't go getting any ideas about escaping."

As soon as Slim Slak was gone Beautron unstrapped herself and began looking around. When she went over to the spaceship door she saw something in a corner, a skycle!

Maybe she could use it to get away. But she had to hurry. She grabbed one of the space suits and helmets hanging by the door and put them on. Then, she jumped on the skycle and started it up.

Beautron heard Slim Slak's footsteps. He was on his way back!

She got even more scared when she realized that she didn't know how to open the door. There was a keypad next to it. She pushed one key, then another, then another.

Nothing happened.

The footsteps were getting closer!

Beautron didn't know what to do. Scared and mad at the same time, she hit the keys with her hand and pushed them all at once.

The door slid open!

Beautron guided the skycle through it. Just as she did her captor was back.

"Hey," he laughed. "What are you doing? Come back here with my skycle."

Then the doors of the spaceship closed behind her. Slim Slak watched her on the monitor screen. He smiled. His idea had worked. Beautron had gotten away.

Beautron flew back towards the planets they had just passed in the spaceship. It was very dark in space and space rocks kept flying past, almost hitting her.

But she flew on.

Then something began to happen to the skycle. The engine began to make noises and it began to slow down.

"Oh no!" said Beautron. "The power cells must be weak. I won't be able to fly much farther."

Beautron was getting close to one of the planets.

"Come on little skycle, just get me to that planet!" she said. Soon she was over the planet. But the skycle kept getting slower and slower and slower. When she was safely through the atmosphere, it stopped.

Suddenly, Beautron and the skycle began falling straight down to the planet. She fell, and fell, and fell...

Oomph! She landed hard, right in the branches of a giant purple pine tree, and was knocked out cold.

Several friendly mechano-monkeys lived in the

purple pine trees. They were very surprised when the beautiful brown woman fell into their trees. They ran over to her and were happy to see that she was still alive.

One of them put Beautron's head in his lap and began to stroke her hair. Two others held her hands.

After a while Beautron woke up. The smiling faces of the mechano-monkeys was the best sight she had seen in a long time. She sat up and smiled back at them.

She felt safe.

"Too bad these mechano-monkeys can't talk," she said. "If only you could tell me where I am. But you can still help because mechano-monkeys are very smart."

"I'll bet you can lead me to where some people are. There are people on this planet aren't there?"

The mechano-monkeys all jumped up and down, making noises and nodding their heads.

"Good my little friends," she said. "Let's go."

The mechano-monkeys helped Beautron climb down from their giant purple pine tree. It was a very long way down.

When they finally reached the ground, Beautron saw nothing but giant purple pine trees as far as the eye could see.

The mechano-monkeys led her through the trees until they came to a clearing. In the middle of the clearing was a very tall and skinny house shaped like a pyramid. The door alone must have been ten feet high.

Beautron followed the mechano-monkeys to the tall door. She knocked. No one answered.

She knocked again.

Still, nothing.

"Hello in there," she called. "Does anyone live here?"

When no one answered this time she pushed at the door and it began to open. She was surprised at how light it was for something so big.

She went inside. The mechano-monkeys followed her.

Inside she saw a tall table shaped like a triangle. At the table were three triangle-shaped chairs. There were also three triangle-shaped plates as large as extra large pizzas.

"Three very tall people must live here or something," she said.

"But where are they?"

She went to the kitchen. Everything was tall! She guessed from the size of things that the people who lived there must have been at least ten feet tall. The triangle plates were everywhere. It looked like the three tall people never washed them, but only used them and threw them into the kitchen sink.

She picked up a plate and was again surprised at how light it was for something so big.

"Maybe if I can climb up into one of their chairs I can wash these dirty dishes for them. Then, perhaps they'll be thankful and help me get back home."

Beautron pulled one of the tall chairs over to the sink. With a mighty jump she pulled herself up into the chair.

The mechano-monkeys passed the plates up to her by standing on each others shoulders. There were so many dishes that they worked for an hour.

Eventually, they were finished and Beautron looked around the house more. She came to a long set of stairs and decided to see what was up there.

At the top of the stairs was a long hallway with a tall triangular ceiling.

Beautron and the mechano-monkeys walked down the hallway. Along the wall were three tall triangular shaped doors.

Inside the first there was long bed also shaped like a triangle. In the next room, the same thing. In the third room, also. When she got to the third room Beautron went inside and sat down on the bed. She was so tired. Pretty soon, she had laid down and went to sleep.

A very large space car soon approached the house. Inside were three very tall girls. All three looked just alike. They landed the space car right in front of the house where Beautron was sleeping.

It was their house.

“Which one of you left that bedroom light on?”

said one.

"Not me," said another one. "Maybe a Rip-Off Rider is inside stealing," the third one said.

The three of them started to get scared. They all climbed out of the space car and went inside the tall front door. As they walked they all tried to hide behind each other.

When they got to the kitchen they could not believe their eyes.

"The dishes are washed," the first one said. "Someone must have been here."

"Maybe they still are," said the second one, trembling.

"Maybe upstairs," said the third.

Holding on to each other tightly the three tall girls went up the stairs

They looked in the first room.

Nothing.

They looked in the second room.

Nothing again.

They looked in the third room.

The sight of Beautron asleep on the bed scared them and they screamed.

Beautron jumped up.

“Who are you?” she said.

“We live here,” one of the tall girls said. “Who are you?”

“My name is Beautron,” she replied.

“I am Speak-Nan,” said one of the tall girls.

“I am See-Nan,” said another.

“I am Sound-Nan,” said the third.

“We are the Titan Triplets,” they all said together.

“You are all so tall,” said Beautron. “But yet you seem so young.”

"We are young," Speak-Nan said. "We are not grown up yet."

"You mean you're STILL growing? You get bigger?" said Beautron.

"Yes," See-Nan laughed. "We are still teenagers and have a lot of growing to do!"

Sound-Nan said nothing. She just listened.

"Come on," said Speak-Nan. "Let's all go downstairs and have some purple pea tea."

Beautron went with the Titan Triplets downstairs. They went to the kitchen and Speak-Nan made some purple pea tea.

After drinking it Beautron felt refreshed. She wasn't tired anymore.

She wasn't even hungry.

"How did you get on our planet?" See-Nan asked Beautron.

The beautiful brown woman told the Triplets about her beautiful sister and how she wanted to kill her.

"Maybe you should stay here," Speak-Nan said. Your evil sister will not be able to bother you here.

"But I want to go back to my home planet," said Beautron.

"If you go back there you will die!" said See-Nan.

"I have to go back," said Beautron. "I have to make my sister see how wrong it is to care more for her own beauty than her own sister!"

"Maybe she doesn't want to see how wrong she is," said See-Nan.

"I have to try," said Beautron. "She's still my sister and no matter what she has done I still love her. I have to make her see that love is stronger than beauty!"

"Well if you must, you must, said Speak-Nan. "What can we do to help you?"

"Do you have a spaceship?" asked Beautron.

"Yes, right out in the back of the house. We don't use it much but it works okay. I think the last time we used it was a month ago when we went to play that game on Timor."

"What game?" asked Beautron.

"A basketball game," Speak-Nan answered. "We all play for the Cosmic Cagers, the best team in the galaxy."

Beautron laughed.

Then the four of them went to the spaceship. When they were inside they all strapped themselves in and Speak-Nan guided the long ship high above the Titan Triplets Triangle House and over the purple pine trees. They were on their way.

"You know," said See-Nan, "once we get to your planet it may be a good idea for the three of us to stay around a while to help you in case your mean sister tries anything."

"Oh, I would like that," said Beautron.

"Besides, said Speak-Nan, "you have no place to go when you get back to your planet. You can't go back to live with your sister until you know it's safe. You can stay on our spaceship until then."

Speak-Nan was right thought Beautron. She did not have any place to go.

When they reached Beautron's home planet they landed their spaceship just outside of the city where Beautron's sister, Beautina lived.

In the short time Beautron had been gone Beautina had become the most powerful woman on the planet. Since there had been no one but Beautron who came close to her in beauty everyone gave her whatever she wanted and did whatever she said.

Each day she sat down in front of her computer. If the computer said that someone on the planet was getting to be as beautiful as she was Beautina would have them removed from the planet.

The day after Beautron returned Beautina asked the computer if she was still the most beautiful woman on the planet.

The computer said no.

Beautina flew into a rage!

“Who is she? Where is she? I'll get rid of her!”

“On the outskirts of town in the spaceship of the Titan Triplets, Beautron still lives. She is the brownest and most beautiful.”

“Beautron! Alive? That’s impossible,” roared Beautina. “If you want something done right you have to do it yourself! I’ll take care of Beautron myself!”

Beautina ran to her room and slid open the closet

door. At the top was a box and she pulled it down.

Inside the box were several disguises. Beautina sat down with the box in front of a mirror. Then she put on a disguise. A man's wig, a mustache, a beard, a man's suit, shoes and a hat.

When she finished she looked just like a very handsome man. Then she put a tiny voice box in her collar and when she talked it made her voice sound very deep.

Then Beautina took a pair of latex lips out of the box.

"These poison latex lips will do the trick," said Beautina. "All I have to do is get Beautron to kiss me."

Beautina hopped into her space car and flew to the Titan Triplets' spaceship.

"Hello down there strangers," called Beautina in her man's voice. "Can you help me?"

"What is the problem?" asked Speak-Nan.

"I was looking for a beautiful girl to have a picnic with and I can't seem to find one. I have all this food and no one to share it with," Beautina answered.

"The only beautiful girls around here are us four," giggled See-Nan.

"Well, well, that would even better," said Beautina, "a picnic with four beautiful girls."

"Come on down," said Speak-Nan.

Beautina came down and the Titan Triplets thought she was the most handsome man they had ever seen.

Beautron thought so too. She never thought for a second that she was talking to her own sister as Beautina spread a large blanket. Then she put lots of delicious picnic food out for them.

"I bet you are the most beautiful woman on the planet," said Beautina to Beautron.

"Thank you," said Beautron.

The Titan Triplets were a little mad that the handsome stranger was not paying any attention to them. One by one they got up and went inside the spaceship. Soon Beautron and Beautina were alone.

"You are so beautiful," said Beautina, "Give me a kiss."

"No I can't do that," said Beautron. "I just met you! I'm not that kind of woman."

"I don't mean a kiss on the lips," Beautina said. "just on the cheek." Surely, you can give me a little kiss on the cheek."

"Well", thought Beautron, "I guess there would be nothing wrong with a little kiss on the cheek."

"Good! Good!" said an excited Beautina. "Kiss me right here on my cheek."

As Beautron bent over to kiss Beautina's cheek,

Beautina turned her head. Before she knew what was going on, Beautron had kissed Beautina's poisoned latex lips!

Suddenly Beautron fell out cold. She was fast asleep!

Beautina jumped up, hopped into her space car and sped off.

"Stay with Beautron," Speak-Nan said to the other two. Like a laser shot she hopped into their spaceship and within no time had almost caught up with Beautina.

Beautina saw she was being chased and got very scared. She lost control of her space car and crashed into a power pole!

That was the end of her beauty.

Speak-Nan returned and found that Beautron had still not awakened from the effects of Beautina's poisoned latex lips. Beautron slept, slept and slept some more. The Titan Triplets watched over her all that time and made a special triangular bed for Beautron to sleep on. They never left her alone.

As the day came to an end a successful businessman named Ronald Romp was out for a joy ride on his new platinum skycle. He saw the Titan Triplets sitting around crying and called down to them.

"What is wrong?"

"Our friend Beautron," said one. "We can't wake her up."

Ronald Romp landed his platinum skycle and came over to them. He told them his name, but said his friends just called him, "The Ronald". The three of them explained how Beautina had tricked Beautron to kiss her poisoned latex lips.

Then he went inside the spaceship with them and saw Beautron.

"Surely, you are the brownest and most beautiful woman I have ever seen."

His heart was filled with pure love for her and he leaned over and kissed her on the cheek.

Beautron woke up!

She smiled at the cheering Titan Triplets and gave Ronald Romp a great big hug!

"Marry me," said Ronald Romp.

"Yes," said the Titan Triplets together as they giggled.

Beautron laughed too.

"Maybe," she replied. "We can wait for that. I think we need to get to know each other better and be good friends first. Then we have a better chance of having a good relationship and a long future ahead."

Soon it was time for the Titan Triplets to return to their home. Laughing and crying at the same time, the four women said their goodbyes.

Beautron climbed on the back of Ronald Romp's platinum skycle and they flew off to his Super Sunnyside Space Station where they looked forward to their long future together.

ABOUT THE AUTHOR

Dr. Ronald L. Washington is a 53 year-old father of four; ages 29, 27, 8 and 3. He started writing children's stories in 1985 to fulfill his child, Oni's voracious appetite for new stories. Since then, he has read these stories, called *"Sleepy Time Space Tales",* to all his children. At the insistence of his 8 year-old daughter Alexis he decided to look into publishing "*Sleepy Time Space Tales*" for other children to enjoy.

Dr. Washington has had a life-long love of writing. In college, he was Senior Editor, Sports Editor (played football, ran track), and Featured Columnist of a column called *"Inside Washington"* for the "*Black Voice/Carta Boriqua"* newspaper." He also wrote, produced and hosted *"Insights and Issues",* for campus radio station, WLIB.

A retired Attorney-At-Law of the State of New Jersey, he now teaches Social Studies at an Atlanta, Georgia high school. He remains a member of the New Jersey Bar, Third Circuit Court of Appeals, and the Supreme Court of the United States. He earned a Juris Doctor degree from Rutgers University-School of Law in 1986, and a Bachelor of Arts in Political Science from Rutgers University in1981.

Made in the USA
Charleston, SC
12 August 2012